Knight

A CLUB ALIAS NOVEL

KD Robichaux

Copyright © 2018 KD Robichaux. All Rights Reserved.
This book is a work of fiction. Names, characters, places, events, and other elements portrayed herein are either the product of the author's imagination or used fictitiously. Any resemblance to real persons or events is coincidental. No part of this book may be reproduced, stored in a retrieval system, or transmitted by any means without the written permission of the author.

Knight Production Crew

Editing by Hot Tree Editing
www.hottreeediting.com

Cover Design and
Formatting by Pink Ink Designs
www.pinkinkdesigns.com

Dedication

For V.
You're here because of this novel.
*grins wickedly

Also by KD Robichaux

THE BLOGGER DIARIES TRILOGY

Wished for You

Wish He Was You

Wish Come True

No Trespassing

Steal You

THE CLUB ALIAS SERIES

Confession Duet (Before the Lie & Truth Revealed)

Seven: A Club Alias Novel

Mission: Accomplished (A Club Alias Novella Boxed Set)

Knight: A Club Alias Novel

COMING SOON

Doc: A Club Alias Novel

Knight

Chapter 1

Brian

"Just send the fucking text, you pussy." Even though my words are whispered to myself, they still sound loud in my perfectly silent bedroom. And although I know I'm alone, I still glance around to make sure there's no one watching me be a total fucking chickenshit. "She's your best friend. You want to spend time with her, even if you don't have a mission at the moment for her to meet you at."

My cell phone screen glows brightly in my pitch-black room, and I almost want to hold it away from myself in case it bites me. Who knew such a small device that I have complete control over could be so intimidating?

"Yeah," I respond to myself, rolling my eyes. "My best friend I'm completely fucking in love with."

I sink deeper into my pillow, my finger hovering over the Send key. "Yep, you'd totally have her babies."

I stare at the tiny circular picture of Clarice in the middle of my screen, her smile vibrant and unmistakable, even in such a small-scaled photo. That smile soothes me just long enough that my hand relaxes and my thumb sends the message through. I gasp like a fucking damsel, but then I see the three dots dancing in response. "Fuck it. The worse she can do is say no, right?" I murmur.

I read my text once again as I wait for hers to show up.

Me: Can I steal you for a while? Maybe not return you until they do an adult Amber alert on you? I could always return you with a "Sorry" sticker :)

My phone makes its little *whomp* sound, and my heart gives an extra hard thump.

Clarice: Steal me? I'm just at home. Where's your mission?

I perk up a little. She's free to meet up like we usually do when I go on one of my jobs as a mercenary. Our schedules normally have this mystical way of lining up together. Either she's near where I'm sent, or close enough that I can grab her on my way to get the job done. We usually spend a couple of days in a hotel together before we go our separate ways, until the next time I'm ordered to kill some motherfucker who deserves much worse than my swift takedown. And in those hotels, we create magic together. We fulfill every need, desire, and craving either of us could ever imagine.

Me: No mission.

I take a deep breath. Do I add to that and risk freaking her out? There's a fine line for Clarice. You get too close to it, and she scampers away like a frightened puppy. She's my best friend, my lover, my goddamn *person*. But if I show how deeply my love for her runs, she shuts me out. And I can't fucking handle that.

Yet…

I decide to go for it.

Me: Just miss you.

There. Oh fuck. The dots dance, taunting me with what she could be replying. Every possible bad scenario flits through my brain by the time her text comes in, so I sigh in relief when I read what she actually sent.

Clarice: Miss you too, big guy :D Where we going then? Florida was fun that time…

Ah, Florida. Yes. Clarice met me down in the Keys for a mission, like she always does—the perks of being a freelance photographer who can make your own schedule—and I'd taken a few days off just to spend with her when I completed it.

Me: Well, I was thinking. Maybe you could come here. To my house. See my club finally.

There's a pause. And in that pause, every nightmare I've ever had of her telling me she finally wants to end everything between us plays through my mind. I'm so deep in self-doubt that when her response arrives, I flinch at the sound.

Clarice: I don't have another shoot lined up for two weeks. I'd love to! I'll bring everything with me just in case a job comes in, but otherwise, I'm all yours.

All mine.

"All mine!" I yell, jumping up in bed like a fucking teenage girl who just got asked out by the boy she's been crushing on. But I don't give a shit how stupid I look. No one is here to see me acting a fool.

And no one is here to help me if I knock my damn self out,

as I feel the top of my head graze my ten-foot ceiling when I jump up and down. Being 6'8", it had been a requirement when I started searching for a home that I have extra high ceilings and doorframes. As I dust the popcorn texture out of my hair and settle back down on my California King, I'm grateful my real estate agent found exactly what I was looking for, or that could've been ugly.

Now that the nerve-wracking part is over, I settle back down into my normal calm, collected demeanor. Anxiety is a foreign emotion for me… unless it has to do with Clarice. That woman. I swear to God, she's more intimidating to me than the most dangerous terrorist. She makes my heart pound harder than being in the middle of a firefight during my deployment. She makes me sweat more than all my mercenary missions combined.

If my partners would've seen me just moments ago, jumping on my bed, they would've had me committed. They've never seen me around Clarice. Hell, they don't even know she exists. The Brian they know is stone-faced, barely has a sense of humor, serious, and 100 percent focused on the job. But little do they know I'm so zeroed in on my missions, because that's the only time for the last several years that I've been able to see Clarice. And when I'm not with her, I'm thinking about her, worried about her out there in the world alone, wishing she was here by my side.

Clarice: Bri? Did you fall asleep?

Me: Far from it. I don't think I'll be able to sleep until you're here. I can't believe you said yes!

While I may hold back from telling her just how much she means to me, I'm always, *always* honest with her. There are no secrets between us. What's the point in having a best friend if you can't confide in them?

Clarice: LOL! I think I've gotten spoiled, getting to see you so often lately. But then when I wasn't able to meet up with you for this last one, it seriously bummed me out. It was... uncomfortable not being there with you, after our adventures in New York, Raleigh, and Nashville.

Her admission makes my chest swell. I know exactly how she feels. It was incredibly lonely in Charlotte without her. I missed the excitement of meeting her at the hotel, the passion of having her top me, the look of delight on her perfect face when I shared with her the details of the job, and of course my reward at the end for completing my mission.

Her submission.

I'm only ever granted that sweet prize, the Holy Grail when it comes to Clarice, whenever I'm finished with a job. Otherwise, it's me who gives in to her dominance.

Me: It wasn't the same without you. When can you come?

Clarice: I have to finish up some edits, and I have a doctor appointment the day after tomorrow. So how about the day after that? Thursday?

Me: Dr appointment? You ok? Thursday sounds perfect.

Clarice: Yeah, just my yearly with my girly doc. Yay! I'm excited.

Me: Me too! I seriously thought you'd say no.

Clarice: You did? How could I ever tell you no, silly?

Me: IDK. But I sure am glad you didn't. Time is going to go by so slow now.

Clarice: Oh, it won't be too bad, big guy. I'm tired as hell, so let's try to get some sleep. See you in 3 days, okay?

Me: Yes, ma'am. Night, lover.

Clarice: ;) <3

I smile as I lie back on my pillow, adrenaline rushing through my veins stronger than when I'm in the middle of hand-to-hand combat with a sex trafficker. But a few moments later, her words remind me of something very important. And I realize I have to

Chapter 2

Brian

The next morning, I sit in the waiting room inside Doc's office. Usually, we catch up at the club, but I needed to see him ASAP to start downloading a bunch of shit he doesn't know.

When Doc, Seth, Corbin, and I formed our mercenary team—which we hid behind a legitimate security company, Imperium Security—one of the rules Doc put in place was that we'd have to attend regular therapy sessions with him. And we always follow Doc's rules. After all, he put our group together.

The door opens, and a middle-aged woman steps out, thanking the towering bearded man behind her for making her feel much better. He gives her a small smile and a nod before she hurries out the front door.

"Come on in," he tells me, and I follow him into his office, plopping down on his couch as he takes a seat in front of me in his chair.

He takes his notepad off the small side table next to him, uncapping his pen. "Needless to say, I was surprised to receive your text last night asking to meet with me. You do realize it's usually like pulling teeth getting you to sit down and share any sort of feelings, right?"

I feel a twinge of guilt. He only put the rule about therapy sessions in place to look out for our well-being. I rub the back of my neck, looking him in the eyes. "I know, Doc. But… I'm ready to share now. Actually, I have no choice but to share now."

"I see." He crosses his legs, placing his ankle on the opposite knee. Leaning over in his chair to place his elbow on the armrest, he rubs his beard. "Are you saying you haven't been honest with me during the sessions you *have* agreed to?"

"Not at all. But our sessions have always been about how I feel about our job as mercenaries. I download everything to you after a mission. You debrief me, making sure killing all the assfucks isn't doing any psychological damage. Or any more, rather." I chuckle, trying to relieve some of the tension in the air.

"And this appointment isn't about that?" Doc lifts a brow.

"Negative. This appointment is about…" I shift in my seat. I'd been in such a rush to prepare everyone for Clarice's arrival that I never actually thought about what I'd say. Fuck. I guess I'm just going to have to be honest here. "This appointment is about Clarice. My… my best friend. Who… I'm in love with."

The look on Doc's face almost pulls a laugh from me. Usually, there's no shaking the man. He stays calm, cool, and collected through some of the most trying therapy sessions with victims of terrible crimes. But right now, his eyes are bulging and his mouth gapes open.

He snaps his jaw shut and sits up in his seat, clearing his throat. "Well. Okay then."

"Yeah."

"I mean, I've never forced you to talk about anything other than the job, because you never partake in any of the club's activities. When Seth initially had the idea to build Club Alias as a backup monetary resource in case Imperium Security didn't do well, and we all chipped in as partners, we talked about previous relationships in our first therapy sessions. It was agreed upon by all of us that in order to be the head Dominants, we had to know for sure we were capable of handling any situation and nothing from our past would get in the way of that," he reminds me.

"And I was honest back then. I told you about the only two relationships even worth mentioning. There was nothing extraordinary. Just two short instances where I dated, had regular ol' vanilla sex, and then we went our separate ways. Relationships in the military are hard. That's why I never really tried to have one," I explain.

"Yet you're saying now that you're in love with someone. Your best friend, you said?" He looks down at his notepad, only to find it empty. Since I shocked him so badly, he forgot to write anything down.

"Clarice," I supply, her name instantly bringing warmth to my chest.

"Clarice." Doc eyes me, and then he smiles.

"What?"

He shakes his head. "Nothing." Then tries to hide his grin.

"What?" I growl.

"I just never… Bri, I thought you might be gay. I mean, not that there's anything wrong with being gay. Nothing at all. But…

I thought you were gay and that you were in the closet, and that's why you never participated at the club," Doc says. "And as it wasn't my place to force you to out yourself. Since it didn't affect your ability to get your missions done nor take care of the club, I never brought it up. Little did I know, you had a… best friend. Who you love."

I can't help but chuckle. "Not gay. Just wrapped around one tiny little woman's finger."

"So why the sudden need to share?" he asks curiously.

"She's visiting me in a few days. It's the first time she's ever come to me, and I want to show her my life here. Introduce her to everyone, take her to the club. And in order to do that, I knew I'd have to open up to you if I wanted to bring a guest."

He nods. "And is she aware of your feelings for her?"

"She'd have to be blind if she wasn't. And one thing Clarice is definitely not is stupid. But she is… closed off to them. Whenever I try to display my love for her, her walls go up. She changes the subject or laughs me off," I explain.

"Well, let's start from the beginning, shall we? How did you two meet?"

I settle into the cushion of the couch, lean my head back, and close my eyes, letting the memory overtake my mind.

Eleven Years Ago
Khost, Afghanistan

"Do you mind if I take your picture?"

At first, I ignore the soft female voice as I take another bite of my dinner. The mac and cheese has gone cold already, but it doesn't matter. It's so blistering outside one wouldn't really want to eat steaming hot food anyway.

"Sir?" comes that sweet voice again, only this time it's louder, with more authority behind it.

I glance up from my plate of orange, sticky noodles and into the most beautiful brown eyes I've ever seen. With my mouth full, my bite half chewed, all I can do is grunt. "Me?"

She smiles, her perfectly white, straight teeth standing out against her tan skin. In fact, that gorgeous, bright grin looks completely out of place in the chow tent. Everything else is dull and dirty, like a painting that's been kept in an attic and hasn't been dusted in decades. It makes you want to take a rag and Pledge the shit out of every fucking thing, but there's no getting rid of moondust.

"Yes, you." She chuckles, and it's a sultry sound that goes straight to my cock.

"Um..." I look around, wondering if this is some kind of joke my superiors are playing on me.

"I work for Sands of Time Magazine. Just taking some shots of soldiers during their daily routines. Nothing big. Thought I could get a good pic of the chow hall," she explains, lifting her giant black camera in one hand from where it had been hanging from a thick strap around her neck.

I swallow my macaroni. "Oh. Well... sure, I guess. Do you want me to, uh...?" I stand up from my seat, and her eyes widen as she peers up at me.

"Whoa, you're a big guy, aren't you?" she breathes, her gaze traveling over me from my buzzed hair to where the lower half of my legs covered in DCUs disappear behind the table. "How tall are you?"

If I had a nickel for every time someone asked me that... "I'm 6'8", ma'am."

She laughs again. "Oh my God, don't call me ma'am. I'm not that old."

"How old are you?" I groan at myself. "I'm sorry. Don't answer that. My mind-to-mouth filter seems to be missing."

"Oh, honey. Don't worry about manners with me. How long do you think I'd survive around a bunch of soldiers if I cared about y'all being couth? I'm twenty-six," she tells me, waving away my rudeness.

"Yeah, probably not very long, or you'd spend the entire time you're here offended." I glance down at my half-eaten dinner.

"How old are you?" she asks, and I look up to find her pressing some buttons on her camera before lifting the viewfinder to her eye.

"Twenty-one," I reply, fidgeting where I stand as she takes a photo. "Do you want me to like… pose or something?"

"No, you can go back to eating if you want. I didn't mean to disturb you. Candid shots always turn out the best, yet I have to have permission for the magazine." She rolls her eyes. "Kind of a catch-22."

I lower myself back onto the bench and grab my fork. "I'll just pretend you're not there." Yeah, right. As if in a million years I could ever ignore her presence. Every word out of her mouth is mesmerizing. I hear the shutter go off a few times as I try my best to look like a badass while eating mac and cheese.

"That's perfect. Thank you…" She holds out the word, and I meet her gaze once again.

"Glover. Brian. Brian Glover," I fumble, closing my eyes briefly and shaking my head at myself.

"Thank you, Brian." Her voice is low and flirtatious as she tilts her head to the side with another one of her gleaming smiles.

"You're welcome, ma'a—um…"

"Clarice," she supplies. And as I lift my brow—0"Yes, like the FBI trainee."

"I suppose people quote The Silence of the Lambs to you as much as people ask me how tall I am, huh?" I smirk.

"Touché, big guy." She winks. "Enjoy the rest of your dinner. I'll see ya around." And with that, she turns with her camera aimed in another direction, snapping random photos as she maneuvers between tables and benches. The swish of her hips is so hypnotic that by the time I lose sight of her, my macaroni has hardened and my Coke has gone flat.

"So she's five years older than you," Doc points out, bringing me back to the present.

"Yeah."

"And you've known each other for eleven years now."

"Yep," I reply, popping the P.

"So you knew her before I even approached you about joining my team."

"I did. She actually helped me make the decision to accept your offer," I confess.

He ponders this for a moment. I can practically hear the wheels spinning in his mind, putting everything together.

Nine years ago, Doc had approached me just before it was time for me to decide whether I wanted to reenlist in the army. He'd read my story in an article in *Sands of Time Magazine*. An article that no longer exists anywhere on the Internet. Nothing about me does.

"Clarice Lorenson. The war photographer?"

"The one and only. Well, not anymore. She's a freelance photographer now," I reply.

"She knows what you do for a living? Not just Imperium Security, but—"

"Everything. There are no secrets between us." My knee starts to bounce, my nerves starting to appear.

"And she knows the type of club we run? She's comfortable

with the lifestyle?" he asks, and I can't help the bark of laughter that escapes me.

"Who do you think introduced me to BDSM in the first place? Why do you think I didn't even bat an eye when Seth wanted to open up the club?"

"So you have a sexual relationship with her," he points out.

"Yes," I state, not wanting to go into detail about the specifics of our… intimate encounters—at least not yet.

"All right then. Well. I don't want to miss anything, so how about we treat this like any other person coming in for club membership? Our hour is just about up, but I can see you again tomorrow and then Wednesday. That should be sufficient enough," he tells me.

"Sounds good, Doc."

"Brian, you are aware she'll still need to go through her own therapy sessions, right?" he prompts softly, and I grimace. "You said she's not really open when it comes to feelings."

There are specific rules in place to become a member of our high-end BDSM club, Club Alias. We open up applications only four times a year, because the process is so extensive. A new applicant must have a sponsor, someone who is already a member to vouch for them, who is responsible for them throughout the entire process. Then they must complete at least four hour-long sessions with Doc. He takes the time to determine whether the person is the right fit for our club. If they pass the Doc test, then they go through a probationary period, and membership costs a five-figure chunk, ensuring only the most serious of Dominants and submissives are allowed in.

Needless to say, the people who are able to afford to join Club Alias are people who want to keep their identities confidential.

Well-respected doctors, lawyers, high-ranking military men and women... all wanting to peacefully enjoy their alternative lifestyle without worry of being outed in the real world.

"Doc, I think we're getting way ahead of ourselves. I was hoping just to bring her as my personal guest. I've been close to Clarice for eleven damn years and have never been able to penetrate those walls she's got around her heart. I don't believe even *you* could get past that fortress," I say low, my voice sounding depressed even to my own ears.

"And in those eleven years, she's never come to see your home. Yet, she's coming now," he says with a small smile, giving me the slightest bit of hope. "I assume you've seen her since your days in the army. What do you think has changed?"

"So, uh, yeah... I see her quite often, actually. Nearly every mission I go on, she either meets me there or I pick her up on my way out," I admit, hoping not to be scolded by my boss for bringing along a distraction on my jobs.

"Don't look so worried, Bri. You always complete your missions flawlessly. Either you're very good at not getting distracted by her company, or she's actually a really good quiet sidekick. Either way, your ability to keep her completely secret from us is surprising."

I run my hand through my hair, pushing it back out of my face where it had fallen over my forehead. I wanted to get it cut, but Clarice mentioned she loves the way it looks long. And whatever my girl wants...

"But we'll touch on that on another day. It's time for my next appointment," Doc says, and I nod, standing up from the couch as he does the same.

"Same time tomorrow?"

"Yep, but I'll see you tonight at the club," he tells me, and my eyebrows lift in surprise.

"Are you actually going to leave your captive at home alone?" I tease.

"Actually, no. Astrid wants to go see a movie with Twyla and Vi. And she's not my captive. She just hasn't found a place to move out on her own that I approve of," he defends, and I smirk, giving him a knowing look.

I reach out and pat his shoulder. "You'll wear her down eventually. What woman could possibly resist a hot doctor with a beard who has locked her away in his mansion to keep her safe? And if not you, she definitely wouldn't want to leave ole Scout dog. One look into those mismatched eyes and no woman would dare leave such a lovable, noble steed."

"Are you sure you're not gay?" he grumbles, and I chuckle, feeling a lot more jovial than I usually am outside of Clarice's presence.

"Fuck you, bro. See you tonight."

Chapter 3

Brian
Eleven Years Ago
Khost, Afghanistan

"No wandering off by yourself, camera girl. Stay with me, and you'll be fine," I hear the General say behind me as we exit our Humvee on the outskirts of the village. All that's stretched out before us is rundown buildings, everything a depressing beige. There isn't a stitch of color, neither in the setting nor on the people milling about. Even their clothes are a dingy off-white. Some of the walls and roofs look like they might've been blue at one point, but years of sunlight have bleached them into a morose gray.

"You really worried about my safety, or you just trying to make sure all my shots feature your handsome mug?" Clarice responds, clearly buttering him up to get away with her sassiness.

The bastard wouldn't even be out here if it weren't for her camera, wanting to appear like he includes himself on missions instead of just sending out everyone who's a lower rank than him. But the second he heard she's here to do a spread for her magazine was the moment he suddenly got his hooah back. He wants to act the part of the king who rides into battle along with his warriors, when really he stays safely back in his fortress, sending everyone else out to do the real work.

"All right, boys. Show me this school. I'm excited to see it," Clarice says to our group, and we immediately fall into position. She's made every single one of us putty in her hands with her beauty and charm. Over the past few weeks, I can only imagine the images she's captured, because she can get even the most bullheaded and gruff soldiers to do what she asks for a shot with only her perfect smile and a glint in those mischievous eyes.

Weapons resting with a three-point sling, my rifle lays against my front for easy draw. Unlike in the movies, we don't walk around with our guns at the ready for extended periods—too tiring on one's arms. Plus, we don't want to scare the civilian population. But we've been trained for countless grueling hours to be able to draw our weapons faster than any gunslinger in the Wild West.

Making our way swiftly but carefully through the alleys between buildings, we make our way toward the school under construction. The American government is building it for the town's children as a show of support for the Afghani people. And of course, the general wants Clarice to capture images of it to put in her magazine. Look! See how nice we are?

When we arrive, Clarice and the general wait outside while the rest of the team secures the building. When we give the all clear, I watch her expression as she takes in all the boxes that must've just arrived. They weren't here a few days ago when another group of us came to do our security check. And when she reads on the cardboard that the boxes contain children's school desks and chairs, her face goes soft before she takes a step back and aims her camera at them. The shutter goes off just as we're ordered to secure the perimeter while they wander the inside, letting her take as many photos as she sees fit.

Even though every cell in my body wants to stay close to Clarice to keep her safe—something that's been happening a lot since that day in the chow hall—I have to follow the command. I go in the opposite direction than everyone else, knowing each of my fellow soldiers will break off into their own route in and between the shitty little buildings. Everything on this side of the village is abandoned and falling apart. That's why it was the perfect place to build the school. It would've been too dangerous for the Americans to erect it more toward the center of town, without a fast escape route that the outskirts provide.

As I turn a corner, stepping quietly into another alleyway, I hear voices inside one of the shacks. Normally, I wouldn't worry too much about it. This is a peaceful village, the people always coming out to say hello and gawk at the camo-covered soldiers. It's another of the reasons they chose this place to build them a school. No, what makes me pause just outside a window of the decrepit structure is the fact the voice I'm hearing has a distinct American accent, as if the person it belongs to lives in the south, maybe Georgia.

The window is high above the ground, but thanks to my height, I easily glance inside. For as big as I am, I've been trained to be quiet as a mouse and can go undetected, which is a good thing, since the people inside are only a few feet away from me.

"Pleasure doin' business with you, pal," the American says, his jeans and button-up looking completely out of place, and I see him shake the hand of an Afghani man. Spread out behind them are crates upon crates, each open to show rifles inside.

My first thought is to barge in and ask what the fuck is going on. But two and a half years in the army tell me to turn around and find my commanding officer. Right before I do that though, the American man pivots, looking directly at the window I'm peeking through, and my eyes meet his, the left one of which has a small tattoo of a bow and arrow, on his temple.

And then, all hell breaks loose.

Behind me, an explosion erupts, so forceful it throws me forward against the wall I was backing away from. The sound makes my ears ring in a way I can't tell if it's human screams I'm hearing instead. My leg tries to give out on me as it starts to burn low on my calf, but I can only think of one thing.

Clarice.

And that thought sends me into action. When I come around the corner of the school building, I hurry inside, searching three different rooms before I find her huddled against a stack of boxes, the general crouched over her, protecting her with his own body. And I take back everything bad I ever thought about the guy.

Shocking me, Clarice springs up, practically knocking the general against the boxes as she grabs her camera in hand, looking a little frazzled but otherwise unafraid. "Go, big guy!" she calls to me, and her order snaps me out of it. I vaguely pay attention as the general calls for the medic as I exit the room.

The next few minutes are a blur, as if I'm running on autopilot. I locate where the IED went off in one of the alleyways the rest of my team was securing. Their bodies—some moving, some not—are lying in various positions, the scene horrifying with its splashes of blood and remnants of the explosive.

"Bright red blood," I remind myself, and then get to work, knowing it's up to me to keep as many alive as possible until the medic gets here.

"Tell me what to do, Brian," Clarice says behind me, and I jerk around, my arm out in a halting gesture.

"No! Stay back. There could be another IED. I've got this," I tell her.

"But, there're so many of—"

"Please. I won't be able to help them if I'm worried about you. Just stay back. For me, okay?" I plead.

She looks like she wants to argue, but finally she nods, and I breathe a sigh of relief as she raises her camera instead. Turning back to the soldier over who I crouch, I see the light in his eyes has gone out, and trying my best to ignore the pain in my heart, focusing on the adrenaline rushing through my veins and remembering my training, I move to the next man. He's still alive, but badly wounded. "Bright red blood," I repeat, and I use my knife to tear off scraps of fabric to tie around his bicep to stop the bleeding near his elbow.

Soon after I get to the fourth soldier, the medic arrives.

The critical control point is determined.

The 9-line is used to call in our location.

Helicopters arrive.

And the last thing I'm conscious of is Clarice's gasp beside me as my big frame finally collapses sideways, and her small arms catching me as she cradles me to her.

"So she was with you the entire time, when probably the most traumatic experience of your life happened," Doc states, bringing me back to the present.

I look around his office, taking in the leather seating, dark wood furniture, and filled bookcases, reminding myself I'm no longer in that godforsaken place. "Uh, yeah." I clear my throat, sitting up and regaining my bearings. I don't usually allow myself to delve into my memories of that day in so much detail. Maybe a flash here and there, but never from the time the day began until my lights went out. Doc and I had skimmed over it in our initial therapy sessions all those years ago. But he got most of the information about the event from Clarice's article, with a photographic recap. She'd kept her distance as I'd asked, but the images she was able to capture were incredible and haunting.

"My first instinct would be to warn you that relationships that spring from traumatic experiences rarely last. But here it is eleven years later, and you are still close," he muses.

"Yeah, the weeks after the IED kinda sealed the deal for me that I wanted to keep her around for the rest of my life," I tell him, and he lifts his brows.

"Care to explain?"

"Like I have a choice," I murmur grumpily, but it's all for show. These are memories I dream about often, in great detail, and willingly recall every moment I got to spend getting to know the most incredible woman I've ever met.

Chapter 4

Brian
Eleven Years Ago
FOB Salerno, Afghanistan

"Wakey, wakey. Eggs and bakey." I hear her sweet voice singsonging to me, bringing me out of my restless sleep. I open my eyes, and there she is, the light coming in behind her, making her look like an angel holding a tray of food. "There're those perdy eyes. Now sit your booty up and eat this plate of breakfast I slaved over myself."

"Clarice?" I croak, and then take in my location. I'm on a cot, surrounded by medical equipment. The tent is way cleaner than the one I've been living in for the past few months.

"Damn, it's like we're living in that movie *50 First Dates*. I should record this conversation so I can just play it for you over and over. But the doctor assures me you'll come out of your short-term memory loss pretty quickly." She comes over and sets the tray on a chair next to me, and then grasps my arm. As she helps me sit up, she stuffs some pillows behind my back to keep me propped up.

My head pounds, and I groan, closing my eyes for a moment. And that's when I feel her soft hand against my cheek, her thumb stroking me there as she says softly, "It'll pass in a second, big guy. It happens every time you sit up."

My eyes open and find hers, and the softness I see in them does something funny to my stomach. "What happened?" I murmur.

"The short version? IED. You're a big hero and saved a bunch of your teammates. They brought you to FOB Salerno to take care of your leg and to keep an eye on your traumatic brain injury. And I've been playing your personal nurse since it happened four days ago."

As she says the words, flashes of the event play through my mind, but it seems more like a movie I watched once instead of something I actually went through.

She lets go and turns to grab the tray, placing it in my lap, and when she lifts the lid, the smell of the eggs and bacon makes my stomach growl in anticipation. "The cooks have gotten used to me taking over their space for a few minutes so I can whip you up a special meal." She whispers conspiratorially, "No one else besides you gets real fried eggs and crispy bacon done on the griddle. They get the powdered eggs from a box and limp bacon they just nuke."

"Over medium is my favorite," I sigh, my mouth watering as I pick up a slice of toast and use the corner to rip open the yoke.

"I know. You told me the day you got here, when they brought you the scrambled crap," she replies, and I look up at her. "And I made it my mission that day to make sure you had every damn thing you needed. After seeing everything you did for all those men, you deserved at the very least to have your eggs over medium instead of scrambled."

I swallow my bite. "I was only doing my job, what I'm trained to do. I don't deserve any special treatment." When she lifts her brow at me, I can't help but smile. She's not the type to take any shit from me, apparently. "But thank you. I appreciate you going through all this trouble for me."

"Trouble? Are you kidding?" She shakes her head. "If you could see the images I captured...." She trails off.

"So show me," I prompt, but she just shakes her head again.

"Doctor said that wasn't a good idea. They want your TBI to heal without causing you any more stress. Something about letting the memories come back organically instead of forcing it."

I adjust my position in the cot, and my leg suddenly throbs. She must see the pain and confusion on my face, because she explains, "Shrapnel in your calf. They were able to get it all out, but it'll take a while to heal. But they said you'll make a full recovery... and have a sweet scar as a trophy."

Suddenly, a memory flashes through my mind—my calf burning as I'm pressed against the side of a building, a window above my head, as the sound of chaos goes on behind me.

A window. I was looking through that window when the IED went off. What was I looking at?

"You okay, big guy?" Clarice asks from the chair beside me.

Try as I might, I cannot remember what I saw through that window. But something tells me it was important. I just can't recall why.

"Yeah, I—"

Just then, a nurse walks in holding a syringe. "Good morning, Specialist Glover. How's that leg treating you?"

"It's throbbing pretty bad," I reply, watching her uncap the needle.

"This'll help," she says, and she pushes the liquid into the IV attached to my arm. "How's that breakfast? Your girl is a bossy little thing. She wouldn't take no for an answer when she asked for your meal a certain way. When they wouldn't listen, she snuck into the kitchen and made it herself. They finally let her have her way the past couple of days since she wasn't hurting anything."

I glance over at Clarice with a small smile, and my neck heats when she corrects the nurse. "I'm not his girl, but he's definitely my hero."

The nurse grins, nods, then heads out of the makeshift room. The hospital here is a bunch of tents that have been formed together to create what would be more like an Urgent Care in the States.

"Shouldn't General Diaz be your hero? He's the one who kept you safe when the IED went off." I take another bite of eggs and toast.

"You remember?" Her eyes go wide and she sits up straight.

I tilt my head to the side. "Yeah, I guess I do. I can remember running back to the school building to find you, and—"

"To find me?" she murmurs, and I continue in an attempt to distract her from the fact that the first thing I wanted to do after the explosion was to make sure she was all right.

"And the rest of the team, I mean. I had gone in the opposite direction as everyone else, to secure the alley we knew wound up in a dead end. And when I ran back to the school, he was using his body as a shield over you."

"Yes, and I am super grateful he did what the contract he signed ordered him to do—to be my escort and make sure I didn't die. But you should've seen yourself, Bri. You were like a damn superhero out there, a fucking machine. After you and the medic fixed up all the injured soldiers, you carried every single one of those men to safety, and then made sure all of them got onto the helicopter. You looked like the Hulk out there, lifting them like they weighed nothing. It's no wonder you passed out as soon as you finally sat down in the chopper," she conveys excitedly, admiration in her eyes. It's a look I've never had directed at me before, and it makes me feel even taller than my 6'8".

After finishing my breakfast, she takes the tray away and plops back into the chair while holding her camera. "You're a lot more lucid today. Ever since we got here, you'd ask what happened, and when I told you, you'd say a few words and then pass out a few bites into your meal."

"Really?"

"Yeah. So I felt kind of bad taking photos of you, knowing you weren't remembering anything. So if you want me to, I'll delete them. It's nothing majorly graphic or embarrassing or anything. Just a timeline I thought I could show you once the doctor said it was all right. I know if it were me and I couldn't remember going through something, I'd like to see it later. Like those funny videos of people coming out of anesthesia when they get their wisdom teeth out. You were pretty boring though. You only told me how pretty you think I am about twenty-eight thousand times," she tells me.

I groan. "I thought you said I didn't do anything embarrassing."

She giggles. "Oh, come on, Bri. What's embarrassing about making a girl covered in desert grime, who hasn't showered in four days, feel like a supermodel?"

"Oh, is that what that smell is?" I grin, and she snatches up an ink pen from somewhere and tosses it at me.

"You shithead," she says with a laugh. "I haven't left your side except to make you gourmet meals, and that's the thanks I get?"

I chuckle and then my face goes soft. "Where have you been sleeping?" I ask, looking around for clues.

"The flap right there opens up to an empty cot. They told me I could use it until they needed it." She shrugs.

"Wow. I don't even know what to say. But… thank you," I tell her sincerely.

"I've already decided we're going to be BFFs, so no need to thank me. A guy who rescues people like a goddamn Avenger is definitely one I want in my court. You're stuck with me now," she says matter-of-factly, and I try to laugh, but it comes out more like a snuffle, and I feel overwhelming fatigue pressing down on me. I register Clarice's hand on my cheek as she whispers, "It's okay, big guy. The meds are just kicking in. Get some rest. Try to remember when you wake up again, sweet man." And then blackness consumes me.

When I wake up, I open my eyes to find Clarice watching me intently. I blink a few times, clearing the fog. "Twenty-eight thousand times? Jesus. Was I just saying 'You're so pretty' over and over again on repeat, or what?"

She jumps up from her seat, and practically launches herself toward me until I'm nearly cross-eyed looking at her she's so close. "You remember what I said earlier?" she breathes.

"Uh… yeah." I take in the little flecks of gold in her brown eyes, and the way they tilt up in the outer corners, my heart starting to beat a little faster at her nearness.

She jumps up with a yip. "BRB, BFF!" she calls as she hurries out of the room. When she returns, she's got a man in scrubs with a clipboard in tow. "He remembers what I told him this morning. That's the first time he's ever gained consciousness and remembered where he was," she's telling him, but all I can do is watch her outward show of excitement. Excitement over *me*.

"See? I told you there was nothing to worry about. It'll all start coming back now. Mostly in flashbacks until he can piece the whole story together," he explains to her before coming to my side. "How we feeling today, Specialist Glover?" He takes out a penlight and hovers over me to flash it in my eyes then writes something down on his clipboard.

"Not too bad. My leg is starting to throb a little bit again," I reply.

"I'll have your nurse bring you more pain meds."

I sit up a little. "Is there anything else she can give me that won't knock me out?"

"Yeah. I can switch you from morphine to 800-milligram ibuprofen."

I chuckle, shaking my head. Eight-hundred-milligram ibuprofen is the military's cure-all for every ailment. "That should be good. Thanks, Doc."

"Can I show him pictures now?" Clarice steps in front of the doctor before he's able to exit, her hands clasped together as she bats her eyelashes. "Pretty pleeeease?"

He glances at me over his shoulder with a look of sympathy before giving her the okay. I have no idea what that look is for though. Why would anyone need sympathy for the most beautiful woman in the world wanting to spend any kind of time with you?

"All right, big guy. Prepare to feel like a badass motherfucker," she chirps, grabbing her camera before scooting the chair as close as she can to me. I tilt toward her as much as possible in my cot, trying not to move my leg too much.

As Clarice begins clicking different buttons on her camera, the nurse comes in, carrying a giant plastic cup with a handle and straw full of water, and a tiny clear medicine cup containing a giant white horse pill. I swallow it down and thank her before she leaves us alone.

"Okay, so I'm going to show you on the little screen on my camera instead of on my laptop. Later, if you want to see them all big and detailed, I'll hook it up. But I figure we can start out small." After I nod, she continues, "All right, here we are at the beginning of the day.

We got there, went into the schoolhouse..."

She narrates her photographs, clicking through them at a slow but steady pace, allowing me to take it all in. I can remember everything clearly from when we were together in the building, and then she gives me time to think, seeing if I can recall anything from when I left her and the general to go secure the area.

"There's a blank spot from the time I left the schoolhouse until the explosion went off. But then I can remember running back to y'all. I saw you were okay. I went in search of the rest of the team. And... found them," I say, my voice lowering. "I remember telling you to stay back. And then it's all a blur, like autopilot kicked in."

"Do you want to see the images I captured when you told me to stay back? I'll warn you they're graphic as fuck, but amazing all the same." She reaches out and places her hand on my bicep, and it's right then I realize that with her by my side, I could face pretty much anything.

"I want to see," I tell her, and she nods, tilting the camera in my direction once more.

As soon as my eyes land on the violent image, an entire alley strung with bodies covered in blood and gore, my heart drops to my stomach at the pain I see on all my brothers' faces. I swallow thickly, but when Clarice tries to hide the screen from my view, I reach out and grasp her arm. "No. I'm good. Show me."

She doesn't question me, seeing the serious look in my eyes. She just nods and continues her scrolling. In every single one, she's captured not only the carnage of the scene, but even I can spot the way she focused on the heroism of the lone soldier working tirelessly to save as many of his fellow infantrymen as possible. In one, she zoomed in on a leg as I tied a makeshift tourniquet above the knee. In another, the focus is on my hands putting pressure on a stomach wound. In all of them, the red blood stands out sharply against the all-beige backdrop.

She flips through more of the photos, and the scene changes as more people come into view. I work alongside three medics who arrived, doing whatever they told me to do. And then I watch in awe as she begins to flip through them more rapidly, making it play out like a movie in stuttered motion. The images she captured while following behind me as I loaded each wounded soldier into the helicopters were the kind that could make even the most hardass man weep.

"So that's everything from the village. The rest are the ones I took while they fixed you up," she explains, before she scrolls through photos of the doctor removing the shrapnel from my leg. There's another of me being helped into my cot. And one of me sleeping. And the final one she lands on is of me looking directly into her lens, a drunk, crooked smile on my face as I give her a thumbs-up.

"Can I see?" I ask, holding my hand out to take her camera. She looks at me curiously before handing it over. I push a couple buttons until I figure out how to take it off viewing mode, flip the big, black piece of equipment around, and hold it far out away from me as I lean in closer to Clarice. "Say cheese," I tell her, and then give my best Blue Steel as I hold down the shutter. Her giggle does something funny to my chest.

"Let's check it out," she says, giving a chin lift. When I flip the camera back around, she touches the little triangle button, and we both laugh when our faces fill the screen. "Perfect." She takes her camera from me, smiling down at the photo for a moment before turning it off and setting it inside her backpack that hangs on the back of the chair. "I'm sending those out later today after I get a few more edited. The couple I sent to my boss made her cry, so she wants all of them back ASAP to do a whole spread."

"Wow. That's like... kind of a big deal, isn't it?" I ask. "I mean, I really don't know much about you, other than you're the beautiful photographer who works for a magazine."

"Ah, I've been upgraded from pretty to beautiful now?" She giggles.

"Psh. Gorgeous is more like it. I'm just trying not to give you a big head. It's probably heavy enough with that amount of dirt in your hair," I tease.

"You're not going to leave me alone until I finally shower, are you?" She narrows her eyes. "Ya know, you're not so clean yourself. I've given you little sponge baths in the past few days, but you could do with an actual submersion of soapy water."

"And a shave," I say, before her words dawn on me. "You've given me sponge baths? Dear God. Just go ahead and burn my man-card already."

"Honey, your man-card is made of diamond. Ain't nothing going to even dent that bitch after what you did out there. And negative on the shave. I like the scruff." She reaches up and strokes my cheek, and I instantly harden beneath my thin blanket. I lift the knee of my uninjured leg to hide my predicament.

"They'll eventually make me shave. Once I break out of this joint, it'll be back to baby face until the next time I go on leave or get out of the army. Then I can grow a sweet freedom beard," I tell her. When she pouts, I ask her, "What did they happen to say about showering, anyway?"

"You're not allowed to get your bandages wet, so they gave us these plastic bags to wrap around it once you're able to get up. They took your catheter out this morning after you passed back out, so if you feel like trying to go to the bathroom or want me to help you to the showers, I can."

"I feel like our relationship is escalating really quickly." I eye her, unsure if I want this perfect woman seeing me at my weakest.

"Don't look at me like that, big guy. Told you. You're never getting rid of me." She stands, pulling back the covers quickly. Thank God my boner had a chance to calm down or she would've gotten quite an eyeful. She pulls the pillow gently from beneath my injured calf and then helps me swing both legs over the side of the cot. "Don't hold back. I may be little, but I'm damn strong. Hidden beneath these oversized dirty clothes are buns of steel."

By her tone, I can tell she's trying to joke around and distract me from any pain I might be feeling, yet I still groan, but for a different reason. "Can we not talk about your buns, pretty girl? I'm trying my best not to pop another woody in this scrap of fabric they've got me in."

Her chuckle is sultry as she helps pull me up to standing. "Another? Yeah, they didn't exactly have anything that would fit a real-life giant. Here. I'll wrap this around you while we walk so no one can see your ass." She grabs the sheet from the cot before circling it around my waist. "Awww!" she coos, and I look down at her with my brow furrowed. "You seriously have the cutest butt ever." Her eyes twinkle evilly.

I groan once again. "I'm really in hell, aren't I? I died during the explosion, and now I'm in hell."

She makes sure I have my balance before taking a step sideways to grab the crutches leaning against the tent wall. "Nah, you just got stuck with a guardian angel with a wicked sense of humor. If I were super sweet, you'd totally get bored, and you know it."

"Fair enough," I murmur, taking the crutches and grimacing at how short they are.

"Um... I guess you're just going to have to crouch down for them to fit into your armpits."

I toss one of them onto the cot and just use the one to help me balance as I slowly follow while Clarice backs out of my room. She reaches out and snatches up the plastic bags she told me about, but continues walking backward, her arms out like a mom ready to catch her toddler who's just learning to take steps.

"You know I would pretty much crush you if I fell, right?" I lift a brow.

"But at least I would break your fall," she says, her eyes concentrating on my feet as I shuffle forward.

I don't know if it's the lingering meds in my system, or maybe the TBI acting up, but her words have a strange effect on me. They choke me up, and I do my best to disguise the emotion behind a mask of focusing on walking. True, she might have a wicked sense of humor, but goddamn, no one has ever treated me so selflessly before. This woman—this gorgeous, funny, talented, wonderful woman—could easily become someone tremendously important to me. And if what she said is true, that I'm never getting rid of her, then I seriously can't see one single problem with that. What person in their right mind would want to get rid of a soul like Clarice?

When we finally make it to the latrine, she takes my crutch and leans it against a sink while I hang onto a wall separating the shower stalls. Before I know what's happening, Clarice is kneeling before me, taking my foot and placing it on her thigh. All I can do is watch, speechless, as she snaps one of the plastic bags in the air to open it up, and then proceeds to wrap up all of my bandages from my knee down with precision. When she's done, I have no doubt that sucker is watertight, if the look of satisfaction on her face is anything to go by.

She hops up, and I murmur a thank-you. She grasps hold of the sheet she wrapped around my waist, but before she can yank it free from the knot she tied, I snatch up her hands in one of mine. Her head tips way back so she can look up at me, her eyes a mix of startled and something else I can't quite place. "I can take it from here," I tell her quietly, but she immediately shakes her head.

"No way. You still have all sorts of painkillers in your system, and there's no way I could live with myself if I let a war hero slip and break his skull open."

She tugs at the knot beneath our hands, and the sheet comes free, our gazes still locked. "I won't slip. I'll hold onto the wall the whole time—" I begin, but she's already shaking her head, her eyebrow lifted in defiance.

"Ain't happening. Plus, you have nothing to be shy about. I've already seen your junk," she informs me, and fuck if I don't feel my face heat. At my expression, she adds, "Sponge baths, remember? Couldn't let you lay around with swamp crotch. I happen to know chafing can be just as irritating and painful as a serious injury."

The smile she gives me then is infectious. "Well, what about you? This whole adventure started because *you* were the one who needed a shower," I remind her, completely joking.

She grins, a wicked glint in her beautiful brown doe eyes. "You trying to get me naked, big guy?"

"At least I'm being a little more subtle about it than you are," I say with a chuckle, squeezing her hands lightly.

She seems to think about something for a minute, and then the look of decision crosses her perfect features. "Deal. If you let me stay and make sure you don't fall and crack open your coconut, then I'll wash up here with you. I mean, it's only fair. I've seen yours, so I'll show you mine."

My jaw drops before I catch myself. "I was only kidding."

"I'm not," she states.

"But… someone could—"

"Nah, I've pretty much caught on to the routine around here the past few days. We're good. And even if someone did come in, I'm only helping you get showered. It's not like we're fucking."

The word coming out of her sweet-looking mouth sends every pint of blood in my body straight to my cock.

I've never in my life been around a woman like Clarice. She has more confidence in her pinky toe than the two women I've dated had in their whole bodies combined. And I know this for certain as she wiggles her hands loose from mine and stands on her tiptoes, her body pressing into mine as she reaches behind my neck. I hold my breath as she unties the gown that barely hangs past my balls, feeling her softness against all my hard plains, and I don't move a muscle as she pulls it down my arms. As I still hold onto the wall, the gown ends up bunched around that wrist, and I barely have time to toss it out of the stall before she closes the curtain, shutting us inside.

Her hands go to the front of her filthy brown T-shirt, tugging it out of the waistband of her even dirtier khaki cargo pants before lifting it over her head. She drops the pants to the floor, and it's then I notice she must've already been barefoot hanging out with me in my room. The thought warms me for some reason, liking the idea of her getting comfortable and making herself at home in my space.

She nudges her clothes out of the stall from beneath the curtain with her foot, leaving her in a black sports bra and colorful underwear. I don't really know what they're called. They're like a short version of men's boxer briefs and are sexier than even the tiniest of thongs.

Turn around, Glover, I tell myself. *You should be respectful and give her some privacy to clean up.*

Her hands pause as she grips the elastic of her sports bra, and she looks at me curiously, her head tilting to the side. "How old are you again?" she asks quietly, teasingly.

I swallow the drool forming under my tongue. "Twenty-one," I reply, trying to force my legs to listen to my conscience still shouting for me to turn away.

She smiles. "Well then, why are you looking at me like you've never seen a naked woman before? Surely you're not a virgin?" I feel her eyes like a blowtorch as they make a path from mine, down to my raging boner, and then back up, and I groan at her little smirk.

"No, not a virgin. But sure've never seen a woman quite like you before," I answer honestly.

"What do you mean like me?" she asks, the smirk changing into a genuinely sweet smile, and she does this little wiggle—fuck me—struggling for only a moment as she lifts the black bra over her head.

It takes me a second to form the word, but when I finally do, it comes out husky and almost pained-sounding. "Perfect."

She lightly chuckles as she takes hold of the elastic of those fucking underwear, and with no hesitation, she slides them down her legs before tossing them out of the stall along with her bra. Without paying me any mind, ignoring the fact I can't for the life of me pull my eyes away, even though I know it's rude as fuck just to keep staring, she turns her back to me to face the faucet and then turns on the water. The showerhead spurts to life, raining down on top of her dark head. I stand there, watching her every move, unable to look away no matter how hard I try. She pulls the elastic out of her hair, and as the water catches the strands, the knot she had it in slowly unravels until her dark hair is nearly halfway to her glorious ass. She was in no way exaggerating when she said she had buns of steel. The perfect globes slightly wobble as she reaches out and shoves the metal button on the soap dispenser attached to the wall, filling her hand with the white liquid that she works into a lather before washing her hair.

She faces me then, getting her front out of the spray so she can soap herself up, and my knees almost buckle at the sight of her hands working their way around her breasts, up and down her arms, across her stomach…. She fills her hands with soap once again, and she washes between her legs, her fingers making quick work beneath the small triangle of black hair before she moves down her shapely tan legs. She spins to face the water, letting her front rinse off as she uses another handful of soap to wash her ass I want nothing more than to take a bite of.

When she's done, I'm all but panting, feeling like the wolf from Roger Rabbit, his tongue rolling out of his mouth when he catches sight of Jessica Rabbit. I'm so hypnotized that I can't even make sense of her words when she tells me, "Your turn."

My brow furrows, and when she grins and shakes her head, I finally understand what she's saying as she fills her hand with soap and brings it over to me, her full hips swishing side to side as she approaches. With her empty hand, she takes hold of my wrist and pulls me toward the water, and I carefully hobble forward.

"You hang onto the wall so you don't slip. I'll do all the work," she says, and all I can do is obey as she reaches above her and tilts the showerhead up to get my body completely wet before turning it to the side so she can begin to lather me up. She starts with my chest then down my abs and around my sides, refilling her hand with soap before her much shorter frame dips under my bicep to circle around behind me and wash my back. But instead of just lathering it quickly, she spends time there, her fingers kneading the muscles, her knuckles working up and down my spine. She lingers at my shoulders and neck, making me groan once again as her hands perform magic.

She spends an eternity turning my aching body into putty, using her soapy palms to clean every inch of skin I own, even so much as running them gently up and down my cock two excruciatingly sweet times, during which I nearly come like an adolescent schoolboy. I reach up and turn the showerhead back to facing me, ducking my head low so she can wash my short hair, and then she runs her hands over me one last time to get all the soap off. I've never felt cleaner in my life. Never felt more taken care of. It's as if she baptized me in this stall in the middle of a war, washing all my sins away, leaving me a new man, one who knows after only one day I will forever watch over her.

"There you go, big guy. Your armor is all shiny again. My very own knight," she says, smiling up at me. I want more than anything to kiss her, and as if she reads my mind, she stands up on her tiptoes and presses a quick yet life-altering kiss on my lips. She must feel the shift in the universe too, because she steps back quickly, her fingertips going to her lips as she looks at me questioningly. But before I can reach out to her, she lets out a nervous laugh. "You stay here a minute. I'm gonna run out and get us some towels and some clothes. Relax under the water for a bit. I'll be right back."

I close the curtain as she hurries out of the stall, and I can hear her pulling towels off the shelving unit.

"Hanging yours on the hook out here. I gotta go find you a new gown. Don't go falling before I get back," she calls, and I murmur an okay.

Already on the brink of orgasm, I take my cock in hand, knowing it'll only take a minute to get the release I desperately need after experiencing the most erotic half hour of my life. I lean my back against the shower wall, pumping my hand up and down my throbbing erection, my head pressing against the painted brick as I close my eyes, remembering every line of Clarice's luscious curves. My toes dig into the rough floor, the shower cascading down on my left leg as I keep my right outside its spray as best I can. But it's when the split second of our first kiss pops into my head that my knees quake, my balls going tight right before I come with a muted grunt. I keep my eyes shut tight as I enjoy every spurt that leaves my cock, reveling in the relief it brings.

And when I open them again, there she is, her eyes locked on my face, her chest rising and falling in short, sharp pants, her face flushed as she bites her full bottom lip. One hand holds the curtain back slightly, and the other holds a fresh towel and gown.

I should be embarrassed. I should be mortified that she caught me jacking off to the thought of her. But the way she's looking at me, with heat in her eyes, like she wishes she could've been the one to give me that release, I feel no shame. I feel her eyes continue to watch me as I wash my hands and my softening cock, and I say nothing as I take a careful step toward her. No words are exchanged as she dries me off, refusing to hand over the towel so I could do it myself. And I let her. I let her take care of me. Feeling worshipped as she kneels to dry my legs and feet. She puts that towel on the floor outside the shower stall and grabs the one she'd put on the hook for me, and then makes quick work of unwrapping the plastic bags from around my calf, drying the last bit of water droplets left. She holds open the gown for me to stick my arm through, and then I see she's got a second one I slide on like a robe, so now my backside is covered too.

She grabs my crutch and hands it to me, and we make our way back to my cot much the same way as before, her walking backward to catch me if I fall. Little does she know though, it's already too late.

Chapter 5

Clarice
Present

"You excited to see me tomorrow?" I ask Brian, his handsome face morphing with his smile as I peek at my phone where I have him on FaceTime. I throw some underwear into my suitcase before turning toward my closet.

"Always. Question," he prompts, and I glance over my shoulder at him.

"Shoot."

"Do you always pack naked?" His voice is gruff, just the way I like it.

"Duh. How else would I be able to try on outfits to make sure that's what I want to bring?" I flip my hair out of my face and turn to reach for a sexy little number I plan to wear for him at his club, making sure to do a little booty tooch in his direction.

He groans. "Fair enough. What time do you plan on leaving tomorrow?"

"Mmmm, I think about 2:00 p.m. It'll take me about three hours to get there. So I should arrive right in time for you to feed me," I tell him, stuffing some jeans and a tank top into the bag.

"That's perfect. Doc wants me to do one more two-hour session with him tomorrow before you get here," he grumbles, and I look up in time to see him swipe his hand down his face.

"Aw, what's the matter, grumpy gills? You don't like having to spill your guts to your friends finally?" I pooch out my lips. "What, are you ashamed of me? Don't want all those cute little submissives at your club to know about me?" I provoke, knowing damn well that's not the case. I just love getting him riled up.

"Fuck no, I'm not ashamed of you. And I couldn't care less what anyone thinks at the club. I've never fucked anyone there anyway," he growls.

I allow myself to absorb his words and let them fill me with the love I know he feels for me, but only for a moment before I shoo them away. It's just enough to get me through the self-imposed loneliness I feel every moment of every day. I know he wants to be with me. I'd give anything to be with him too. But I can't. The second I were to finally give in to our feelings for each other would be the second he signed his own death certificate.

He doesn't know the reason I keep him at a distance. He has no idea why I give him my body, my 100 percent devotion, everything but the title and the pretty words that go along with it. It's the one thing I've never shared with him. In the eleven years we've been best friends, we've never once kept secrets from each other. But I've never revealed my darkest truth. Because it would be pointless. He'd only try to convince me it was all in my head, and I'd end up giving in like last time, and then I'd lose the one person in this world I could never live without.

"What did y'all talk about today?" I ask curiously, packing the last of my toiletries.

"I told him about the day the IED went off. And then about the first few days after, when you took care of me at the hospital."

"The Cliff's Notes, or like… did you tell him everything?" I smirk, wishing I could've been there to hear Brian tell the story. I'd love to know what he remembers from that time over a decade ago. I wonder if he recalls every single detail of every single second like I do.

"I spent two hours recalling two days. The day of the IED, and then the day I started remembering what happened," he tells me, and I put a dreamy look on my face.

"Ah, the best shower of my entire life. Who knew it could feel that good just to wash sweat and dirt off your stanky body?"

"I remember it feeling good for an entirely different reason," he says low, and I glance at my phone to see him smiling to himself as he uses his pocketknife to clean out from under his fingernails.

"You told him about that?" I question, surprised he was willing to share something so personal with one of his guy friends.

"What? That you caught me cranking one out? Yeah." He shrugs. "I made a deal with him. You can come to the club as my guest, which is normally not allowed, but you still have to do the sessions. We *both* have to spill our guts to Doc. It's our number one rule that's nonnegotiable. By me telling him all this shit, let that be a clue of how much I want you to come with me." Panic fills me for a moment, but then he chuckles, distracting me. "You should've seen his face. I've never seen Doc shocked before. When I told him who you were to me, he said he thought I was gay."

I throw my head back and laugh so hard tears start to escape the outer corners of my eyes. "Are you serious?" I get out, trying to catch my breath.

"Told you, babe. None of them have ever seen me with a woman. Not once. In all the missions I've done and you met me on, they never knew you were there. You were my little secret. I had you all to myself," he says warmly.

"You seemed to like it that way. You sure you don't want to keep me hidden away?" I ask, half hoping he'll have a change of heart so I don't have to talk to Doc.

"Negative. Because the only thing that could be better than you as my secret lover would be you on my arm, getting to show you off at *my* club. I can already picture everyone's faces. The shock that I'm there with anyone to begin with. And then the absolute jealousy that you're not there with them instead."

I love how honest he is with me. He shares every thought that enters his head. Except for anything delving too close to love. I've trained him well. He knows I'll shut down if he talks about it. Lust, on the other hand… lust I can handle.

"I like it when you get all caveman, Bri. You're pretty damn hot," I tell him, reaching for my sleep tee. I slip it on over my head, letting it fall to midthigh. "I do have a question for you though."

"What's that?"

"You're a *Dom* at your club. Have you thought about catering to our *other* needs?" I pick up my phone and fall back on my bed, holding it above me to look up into his beautiful blue-green eyes.

"As a matter-of-fact, I have," he replies.

"Oh yeah? Pray tell what you've come up with," I urge, giving him a smile.

"Well, I'm going to tell Doc everything. And then I'm going

to see what he has to say about it," comes his answer, and I lift a brow.

"That's it? You're gonna ask Doc?" I giggle.

"Hey, Doc is one pretty fucking smart guy. He's like… the older brother none of us had. I mean, he already thought I might be gay. He wasn't too far off if you think about it." He shrugs.

"Letting a woman control you isn't anything like being gay," I argue.

"Some men would find it very emasculating, lover."

"Do you?" I ask, my heart sinking a little, hoping that all this time, I hadn't been making him feel less as a man.

"Fuck no. I love it when you top me. But I'm just saying, as far as the club goes and how they only see me in the Dominant position, I'm going to see what Doc has to say. Gotta make sure it's not going to fuck up any contracts or something if I let the members know I'm also submissive. It could confuse them, like… how they would speak to me."

"What do you mean?" I ask, rolling onto my side and propping my head up on my hand.

"Like, would the Dominants then speak to me like a submissive instead of their equal? Would the submissives not feel like I'm unable to keep them safe if something goes wrong with a Dominant? That sort of thing," he explains.

"Ah, gotcha. And what about us?" I question.

"What about us?" he asks, a hint of worry in his tone.

"Usually, I top during your mission, and then we switch as your reward when it's complete. There's no mission this time. So how are we going to decide who's in control?"

His mouth opens and closes a couple times, not knowing how to answer. Finally, he says, "I guess I could talk to Doc about that too."

I laugh lightly. "Don't get your panties in a twist, big guy. I'm only teasing. I figured we could either take turns, or to save everyone from any confusion, I could top while we're at home, and you could still be your fully Dominant self at your club. Or, fuck it. We could always fight for the position," I tell him with a wicked grin.

"You think you could take me, little one?" he asks, a smile in his voice as he leans closer to the phone, his tone all deep and sexy and giving me chills.

I bite my bottom lip then lick the top one. "Oh, I could totally take you, big guy," I purr.

"Fuck me," he growls, reaching below the camera's view to adjust what I know is a very blessed package.

"Plan on it," I chirp. "Anyway, I gotta get some sleep. Gonna wake up early and finish some edits, and then I'll be heading your way."

"All right, beautiful. Text me when you're leaving," he orders.

"Will do. Night." We hang up, and I roll onto my back, staring up at my ceiling for a long while.

When he asked me to come stay with him and see his club, I immediately said yes. Because there's nothing in this world I want more than to spend every spare second I can with him. It was my knee-jerk reaction. But now, half of me is regretting it.

When we meet up for his missions, we're on even ground. It's neither of our territories. We're in a hotel, somewhere away from where each of us lives, surviving out of suitcases. Nothing is personal except for what our bodies share. I'm so scared that once I step into his space, not only will Brian feel like home, like he always has, but his actual *home* will feel like home. And it will be so much harder for me to leave. So much harder for me to keep my walls up.

So much harder to keep him safe from me.

Chapter 6

Brian

"You seem anxious today," Doc tells me, and I realize my knee is bouncing. The irritating squeak of leather is my own damn fault. I halt the movement and try to relax into the couch inside his office. "Are you usually this way before you see Clarice?"

I shake my head. "No. I'm usually excited, a little anxious to get to her. But I feel like I'm gonna fucking blow a gasket today waiting on her to get here," I answer honestly.

"Why do you think that is?" he asks in his therapist's voice, putting his pen into position on top of his notepad.

"I don't fucking know." I run my hand through my hair. "Everything, I guess. Will she like my house? Will she like my club? What will she think of my friends? Just… everything."

"Her opinion matters a lot to you," he states.

"Her opinion is the *only* one that matters to me," I correct, looking him dead in the eye.

He looks into his lap to jot something down. "What do you think would happen if she didn't like your house?" he prompts, and it makes me stop to really think about it.

"I…." I pause, and then restart. "She's… she's optimistic. She's very laid-back and just goes with the flow. Honestly, I think she'll really like my house. We have the same taste in a lot of things."

"And the club?"

"She went with me to a lot of the clubs I visited when deciding what to use and what not to use for Club Alias. When you, me, Seth, and Corbin had our meetings about all our findings, a lot of my notes were her point of view, since I thought it'd be good to get the female perspective instead of just us guys." I ponder on that for another moment. "And we always find a local BDSM club to visit after every mission, so I have a really strong sense of what she likes and dislikes about each of them. I think she'll love ours."

"And your friends?"

I can't help but smile. "Now that I think about it, I know she's going to love you guys too. Seth especially. Since I have to work with him on the phone a lot during my missions, she's heard him on speakerphone. And you know Seth. He can't just answer your damn questions and end the call. That fucker's got to joke around and shit. I'm surprised he's never heard her giggling in the background before." I rub the back of my neck. "She's always been curious about you. She knows you found me through her article, and she was there from day one, when you contacted me and asked me to join your team. She's got you up on a pedestal, like the leader of a team of superheroes."

He smiles slightly and shifts in his seat. "I don't know about all that—"

"Cut the shit, Doc." I interrupt his usual modesty. "You know you're a badass. Fuck off. This is supposed to be about me." I chuckle.

"Fair enough. And what about Corbin?" he asks.

"That should be interesting, to say the least." I grin.

He looks at me curiously. "Why's that?"

"Corbin met her in Afghanistan. I don't know if he'll remember her or not. It would've been around the time he got that call from Vi," I reply.

He grimaces and nods. "Ah, yes. Have you kept Clarice updated with all that?"

"Of course. When you, Seth, and I decided to add Corbin to our team, she questioned me repeatedly whether I thought it was a good idea or not. He was a real hothead, pretty insufferable back in the day, and she witnessed it firsthand. But she was very happy to hear that after ten years, he finally got the love of his life back. And now she's excited to see how he's changed."

Doc sits up straighter in his chair. "Now that's a story I'd like to hear."

"Well, as it so happens, that's the beginning of where you wanted me to pick back up today."

"Well, perfect. And since I think you've finally realized you have nothing to worry about as far as her liking your house, club, and friends go, let's proceed, shall we?"

Damn Doc and his fucking brilliant diversion tactics. I roll my eyes at my inability to see what he was doing the whole time we've been talking. But with my anxiety now at a minimum, I begin to speak.

Eleven Years Ago
FOB Salerno, Afghanistan

"They wanted me to feed you some shitty-ass dog food they were trying to pass off as—" Clarice halts midsentence, carrying in a tray with my dinner on it, like she's done for every meal the past week and a half, seeing I'm not alone in my room in the same small clinic I've been in since the IED. "Oh, sorry! Didn't mean to interrupt," she says, smiling at Corbin.

He looks from her back to me, lifting a brow. "I wasn't aware they allowed American civilians to play nurse when they came to do a different job entirely." His voice is full of irritation.

"They're short on staff. Most of the doctors and nurses had to go to the bigger hospital to care for the soldiers hit by the IED. They allowed her to stay here until I'm ready to be discharged, as long as she doesn't leave the clinic without a commanding officer," I explain.

He turns to Clarice, and I can't see his face, but if her reaction to it is anything to go by, it can't be a pleasant one. "Well, isn't that nice? Women all over the world breaking the rules and getting whatever they want, not caring about the consequences or who they may hurt in the process," he seethes and then faces me once more. "You'd be better off taking care of yourself, Glover, instead of becoming used to someone else being there for you."

His face is angry, but I can see the pain in his eyes. Without thinking, I reach out and grasp his arm. "I was there the day you met her, Corb," I speak low, so no one outside the flimsy walls can hear. "I was at your wedding. Vi loves you more than anyone I've ever seen love another person. There's no way, man. There's gotta be something wro—"

He jerks his arm free, cutting me off. "It's Sgt. Lowe, Specialist," *he snaps, and even though it shouldn't—since he is my higher up—it hurts, because, before he got that call from his wife a couple months ago, he was my best friend. He's the one who pretty much taught me everything there is to know about being a soldier in the U.S. Army. He's been there for me since the day I stepped off the bus from boot camp. Yet, he won't allow me to be there for him during a time that would kill a weaker man than Corbin Lowe.*

Without another word, he brushes past Clarice and leaves, nothing but agony written all over his features.

"Geez, who pissed in his Cheerios?" *she asks, finally coming in all the way and setting the tray in my lap.*

Instead of plopping down into the chair like she's been known to do, she walks around to the other side of me and slides into the other cot she'd highjacked from the empty room next to mine. She'd set it up a few days ago right next to the one I lie on, telling me she sleeps better knowing all I'd have to do is nudge her if I need her throughout the night. I swear, this woman.

"He a member of the He Man Woman Hater Club?" *she adds, stealing a roll off the tray.*

I shake my head. "He recently separated from his wife. Something that absolutely blows my fucking mind. It just doesn't make any fucking sense."

"Why? I heard what you said to him. What's the story?"

I spend the next several minutes telling her all about Corbin and his sweet wife—well, soon-to-be ex-wife. But seeing the way it confused and upset me, considering how they were some of my closest friends, Clarice changes the subject several times, while we both eat dinner, until I completely forget about the not-so-great visit from Sgt. Lowe.

"Smithfield's," *I reply, answering her question of where the first stop after my deployment is going to be.*

"Like... the barbecue joint?" she questions, her face scrunching up.

"Fuck yes. You bet your sweet ass I'm going to devour like four of their pulled pork and coleslaw sandwiches." My mouth waters just thinking about it.

"Not what I was expecting. But I guess real food will be high on my priority list too," she concedes.

"What did you expect?" I prompt, nudging her lightly with my elbow.

"Oh, I don't know. A porn shop, maybe, seeing how that shit is illegal here." She chuckles. "Or even better, a bar to pick up some chick. I bet that line works great." She drops her voice low, mimicking a deep male tone. "Hey, baby. I just got back from a deployment, fighting for our country. Wanna make it with a real-life hero who hasn't seen a pair of tits in a year?" She cackles, and I look at her with feigned disgust.

"There is so much wrong with everything you just said."

"Yeah right. How?" She pokes me in the ribs.

I playfully swat her hand away. "One, that's a no on the porn. I don't need to spend money on that shit when I've got better material in my spank bank." I tap a finger on my temple. "Two, I don't pick up chicks at bars. I happen to have a pretty high level of respect for women and have never had a one-night stand." Her eyes widen at that, and she looks like she's about to ask something, but I cut her off. "Three, it wouldn't be a year since I saw a pair of tits, because I've seen yours like five times now," I remind her, and she throws her head back and laughs. Exactly what I was aiming for. I fucking love it when she laughs. She does it with her whole body, shaking while her face alights, filling the whole clinic with noise and joy.

"Okay, okay. Rewind. You've never had a one-night stand

before?" she questions, and I shift a little in my cot. We've talked about nearly everything under the sun this past week and a half, but our conversation has never delved much into the sexual category. This is surprising, now that I think about it, especially since we've showered together several times, and she caught me masturbating.

"No," I reply.

"And you're not a virgin. So... what? Tell me everything," she probes, flipping onto her stomach and propping herself up on her elbows. "And don't play hard to get. Kiss and tell, big guy."

"You're a nosy little thing, aren't you?" I lean over and put the now-empty tray on the chair, and then roll onto my left side to face her, scrunching up my pillow between my head and shoulder. "There's really not much to tell you. I've been with two girls. Well, women. Whatever. I lost my virginity my junior year of high school to my girlfriend at the time. I must not've been very good, because we never did it again after that. We broke up soon after, couldn't tell you why."

Her brow furrows. "Was she a virgin too?"

"Yep."

"Ah, well that explains it." She nods like she's come to some conclusion.

"What explains what?" I ask, watching her smile form.

She props her chin on her hands. "She didn't know she'd struck gold."

"Still not following." I poke her side like she does me, making her squirm.

"Um, hello? You're 6'8" with a dick that's well proportioned with the rest of you. And you used that monster to take a girl's virginity. She probably thinks you scarred her for life, when in fact, she will regret not hanging on to you once she sees what else is out there."

She says it so nonchalantly, like she's talking about the weather, that I just stare at her and blink. There are no words.

She thumps me lightly on the forehead. "Did your brain just short-circuit?"

I swat at her hand again. "You kind of just blew my mind."

She giggles, and I feel the sound hula-hooping around my heart. "Geez, Bri. You're so sweet it makes my teeth hurt. Did you really not consider…? No. Of course not." She shakes her head. "You would think she dumped you because of something you did wrong. Not because she couldn't handle all of what God blessed your hot ass with."

This makes me grin. "You think I'm hot?"

She groans, grabbing her pillow and hitting me with it before stuffing it under her chest. "Have you looked in a mirror… like ever? Besides the fact that your height automatically gives you an advantage above most men—pun completely intended—you've got those killer eyes with lashes I'm severely jealous of. The scruff you're rocking? Panty-melting. And even when you're shaven… bro, you could carve things with that jawline. Brad Pitt could use you as a jaw double. And a lip double, in fact. You and ya damn pillowy lips. They're like a fucking Target ad." She sings in a hypnotist's voice, "'Look into my eye,' the bull's-eye says. 'Come buy all the things you never knew you needed.' But it's your fucking lips instead. 'Come over here and kiss me, Clarice. Come press your lips to the sexiest pair you've ever seen on a guy. You know you want to see what it feels like.' And so I did. And they were magical little—"

I can't stop myself. I shut off her tirade, slamming my mouth down on hers after lunging across the short space between the wooden frames of our cots, and the rest of the world ceases to exist. This isn't the short and sweet little peck we shared in the shower that first time. No. This is the kiss all other kisses will forever be compared to. She whimpers as my tongue parts her lips to dance with hers, and I deepen the caress, *rolling her to her back so I can delve even deeper.*

It's not until her leg wraps around my injured one as she tries to pull me closer that I suck in a breath at the sudden sharp pain. I want to kick myself for being such a pussy, because the sound makes her pull back to look into my face to see what's wrong. She must realize her position, because she jerks her leg back.

"Oh my God, Bri. I'm so sorry. I wasn't thinking," she whispers, and I shake my head, leaning forward to continue our kiss, but she sits up abruptly to check on my bandaged calf. "Fuck. I'm so sorry, big guy. I—"

She looks about ready to burst into tears, so I wrap my arms around her and lie on my back, pulling her down until she lies in my cot with me, snuggled to my side with her head in the crook between my shoulder and chest. "I'm all right, pretty girl. Don't worry about me." I stroke her hair, trying to soothe away the tension I feel coiled in her limbs. "Shh, beautiful. I'm okay. I'm invincible, remember? A goddamn superhero, you called me, right? Your tiny little leg bumping my booboo ain't no thang," I tease, and I finally feel her relax, melting into my side.

Just when I think she's fallen asleep, her sweet voice comes quietly. "So who was the second?" she asks, and it takes me a minute to realize she means the second woman I'd been with.

"My senior year of high school, I had a girlfriend I was really close to. But we wanted different things out of life. We stayed together through that summer after graduation, and then she went off to college and I joined the army. There wasn't any big drama or anything. We enjoyed our time together, and then we went our separate ways," I tell her, and she tilts her head back to look at me.

"I take it your anaconda didn't scare her off," she probes with a smirk.

I let out a bark of laughter before shaking my head. "Nah, she didn't seem to mind it."

"Atta girl." She winks. "So that's it? You haven't been with anyone since you joined the army?"

"No. I never thought it would be a good idea to try to have a relationship when you pretty much have to be married to your job. Having to be away months and even a year or more at a time… that didn't seem the best environment for a lasting relationship, and I'm the kind of guy that if I know it's going to fail from the beginning, then I won't start it. Why put yourself through all the hardship, when you know you're not going to turn up the winner?"

She furrows her brow. "Haven't you ever heard it's better to have loved and lost than never to have loved at all?"

"Yeah. And that's bullshit. I'll avoid the heartbreak and just focus on what I know I'm supposed to be doing," I tell her, although that doesn't seem quite right. Because I'd take a chance on Clarice, even not knowing if it would last or not. I'd be willing to take the chance of us failing if it meant I'd get to be with her for any length of time. But she's special, unlike anyone I've met before, and treats me differently too.

"I can definitely respect you on that one. I'm the same way," she replies, taking me by surprise, especially after her last question.

"Really? Well… what's your story? I told you about my past, so what about yours?"

She cringes, shaking her head. "Like you said, not much to tell. Well, on the relationship aspect."

When she doesn't continue, I nudge her. "Care to elaborate?"

For the briefest moment, I see pain in her eyes, but she quickly disguises it with a laugh. "I don't do well with committed relationships. I'm more a free spirit. If I were in a relationship, I'd have to discuss things like… wanting to run off to Afghanistan to photograph the war.

And I'm sure it'd be hard to find a guy who'd be okay with something like that."

"Fair enough. You're an independent woman. That's hot as hell in my opinion." I smile down at her. "But what about the other aspect though?" I lift a brow.

She plays coy. "What other aspect might you be talking about, Bri?"

I usually hate it when people try to give me a nickname, but I love how she shortens my name, just leaving off the second syllable. It makes me feel like we're closer than what the actual amount of time we've known each other would normally allow. "You're gonna make me spell it out? You won't just let me respectfully hint at what I'm asking?"

"What's the fun in that?" She giggles.

I shift a little, turning my body more toward hers. "All right then." I muster up the confidence I usually have around women and push away the fumbling schoolboy Clarice brings out in me. And even though it goes against everything my momma ever taught me about being a gentleman, I forge ahead. "There's no way a sexy, self-assured woman, who doesn't hesitate to get naked with a man she barely knows, would be a virgin. So tell me, pretty girl. Who have you allowed to sample the perfection I got to see in the shower?" I reach up and trace her full bottom lip with my thumb, watching her eyes go half-mast.

And right when I think I've shaken off the fumbling schoolboy, here he comes rearing his dorky little head, as she opens those fantasy-inducing lips and sucks my thumb into her blazing mouth, looking me straight in the eye as she swirls it with her tongue before letting it go with a pop.

And I think I just came.

"I've got a few years on you, big guy. Five, actually. And let's just say you can fit a lot of experience into five years," she answers vaguely.

When I can speak without my voice croaking like I'm going through puberty, I ask her quietly, "So more than two then?"

She grins. "Yeah. More than two. I would corrupt the shit out of you if given the chance."

I chuckle. "I don't know about all that. You look too sweet to do too much damage."

"Looks can be deceiving."

The way she says it makes me pause. Makes me believe her.

I stroke her cheek and her eyes go soft. "What happened to you, little one?" I whisper, searching her face.

There's a pregnant pause, in which she looks like she's trying to dredge up the courage to confess something monumental. But then she smiles and shakes her head, giving a little shrug. "Nothing happened to me. I'm just a kinky kinda chick. Always have been."

Not wanting to scare her off, when all I want to do is keep her close, I don't press her. In the past week, she's shared with me all about her family, who live in Florida, far away from her home base in New York. She told me how she became a professional photographer who was highly sought after by the popular magazine she works for now, and how she doesn't even rent an apartment because she's never in one place long enough to call somewhere home. She has an office at the magazine, where she installed a Murphy bed and stores her meager belongings. It was in her contract when she took the job that she could stay on the premises whenever she was stateside. And since there was a full gym on one of the floors, she just keeps all her toiletries and such in a locker and showers there.

So instead of urging her to tell me more about her past relationships, I follow her change in subject, since she seems much more comfortable talking about sex. "What do you mean kinky?"

"Oh, lots of different things. But mostly, I like to be in control," she replies.

"Control? Like... what? A dominatrix or something?" My eyes widen.

"Are you thinking of Lucy Lawless à la Eurotrip? You picturing a chick dressed in all red latex named Madame Vandersexxx, yelling for her subs to administer the testicle clamps?" She giggles at my expression. "That's not my thing. I like control, but I'm not big on pain... well, giving it at least."

I swallow thickly. "But receiving it?"

"A little spanking never hurt anybody... too badly." She smiles widely. "You're looking at me like I just stole your lunch money." She shrugs again. "Vanilla sex just doesn't do it for me. There's no big mystery. The physical act of doing the deed just doesn't get me off. But the second I was introduced to BDSM, I set off like a rocket launcher."

I reach down between us and adjust the tent beneath my gown. "Ya know, when I met you that day in the chow hall, I detected a hint of... bossiness? No, that's not right. Authority. Yeah, that's more like it. I heard authority in your voice when you were trying to get my attention for the picture. It's why I looked up. Otherwise, I would've just ignored you."

She bites her lip, her eyes going dreamy. "Such a big man who willingly follows orders and respects women. Oh, the things I would do to you," she murmurs. We stare into each other's eyes for what seems like an eternity, neither of us wanting to break the spell we've put ourselves under. Finally, she commands, "Kiss me," and without a moment's hesitation, I do.

I kiss her like my life depends on it, and when she grasps hold of my hospital gown and tugs it up, I continue alternating between nibbling at her lips, sucking on her tongue, and pressing my mouth to hers, because she never told me to stop. Not even when she grips my cock tightly at its base before stroking upward. Not even when she uses her palm to spread the sticky precum around its crown. Not even when she orders me to "Feel how wet you make me."

But before my hand gliding up her soft inner thigh can reach the heaven I know it's about to find, Clarice pulls away abruptly, hopping into her own cot and reaching over to tug my gown down before I even realize what's going on.

Right then, a nurse walks in carrying a little plastic cup containing one of the giant ibuprofens. "How ya feeling tonight, Glover?" she asks, and when I roll onto my back, I lift my leg a little to obstruct any view of my still raging dick.

"Feeling good," I reply, having to clear my throat as images of what just happened flash behind my eyes.

"Wonderful. Shouldn't be too much longer until we get you out of here," she says like she's delivering the best news ever.

But in my mind, it's not the best news ever. Far from it. Which makes me feel guilty as fuck. Two of my friends died in that explosion. Six more had to be transported to a medical facility far away from this little clinic I'm in, just to have the equipment needed to save their lives. I should be itching to get out of here, ready to get back to work. But here I am, irritated that I'm healing enough to be released, all because I'd rather stay right here in this little room with this tiny woman who makes me feel things I've never felt before.

And the guilt reminds me: this is why I never wanted to be in a relationship while in the military. This is why it would never work between a woman and me while I'm supposed to be focusing on fighting for my country. There's no way to balance the two. I can't split my attention, because that could get me—and others—killed in the line of duty. But if I put all my concentration on my job, that would leave my partner feeling neglected and unloved.

"You okay, Bri? You look about ready to throw up," Clarice says *gently, placing her hand on my arm.*

I look at where she touches me, and then up into her beautiful face, and after a moment, I give her a small smile. "Yeah, I'm all right."

"Well, your vitals look good, so unless you need me for anything, I'm going to get some sleep. Feel free to wake me up if you need me," *the nurse tells us, and we each murmur a goodnight.*

When she leaves, Clarice moves back into my cot, taking hold of my gown once again, but I grasp her hand, stopping her before she can pick up where we left off. "Wait, pretty girl."

"What is it?" *she breathes, leaning up to kiss me gently.*

Keeping hold of her hand, I slide my other one up the back of her neck and into her hair, curling my hand into a loose fist to keep her still. If I allow her to kiss me again, I know I'll forget everything going on in my head. And it's important.

"Clarice, I…" *I look back and forth between her beautiful chocolate eyes, watching her pupils swallow up the brown for a moment before it recedes a little as lights turn off and then on again in the clinic. It's a warning the nurse gives every night before she disappears for a few hours of sleep, letting us know the lights will go out in five minutes. It makes me realize how lonely it would've been here without Clarice to keep me company, people only coming in and out quickly to get stitches or to get bandaged up for minor injuries. I would've been here by myself the whole time, with nothing to do but stare at the tent walls. It would've been miserable. I would've been dying to get back out there in the midst of war. So maybe they do it on purpose, so soldiers don't get too comfortable and want to stay.*

"Brian?" *she whispers, pulling me back from my thoughts.*

"I'm sorry. I'm just… confused," *I confess, and she relaxes against me, the weight of her a comforting presence.*

"Talk to me, big guy. You can tell me anything. I won't share any of your secrets," she promises.

I take in her delicate features, perfect even without the amenities of home. Her face is bare of any makeup, her eyebrows thick but naturally arched. Her skin is flawless in my eyes, even with her light freckles and beauty marks here and there. She's absolutely gorgeous here in this godforsaken country, with nothing but soap out of a metal dispenser to help. I wonder what she looks like when we're back home, when she has access to fancy shampoos, makeup, and civilian clothes.

I hope it's not too different.

"When the nurse said I'd be out of here soon, I wasn't happy about it," I tell her, and she furrows her brow. "I'm supposed to be dying to get out of here so I can kick some fucking ass, but instead, I want to stay holed up with you."

She smiles gently. "You shouldn't feel bad about that, Bri. You deserved a little vacation after what you went through. You earned it when you helped save all those guys."

"I was just doing my job. It's what I'm paid to do. It's what I signed up to do. I didn't commit myself to the army just to get here and hide away while everyone else does all the work," I say, shaking my head, angry at myself.

She swallows, looking a little hurt, but she hides it quickly. "Are you saying you wish I hadn't stayed here with you?"

Her question makes my grip on her hair tighten, and her eyelids dip with what looks like pleasure. "Fuck no. This has been the best almost two weeks of my life, even though I don't remember the first few days of it." I smile, trying to ease her tension. "But now that I'm about to be cleared, I need to get my head back in the game. If not, something bad could happen."

"I can understand that." Her gaze dips to my lips and then back up to my eyes. "But like I said before, you're never getting rid of me.

You know more about me now than anyone ever has. I can honestly say you're my best friend, seeing how all we've done for the past ten days is talk. I've never told anyone as much as I've told you."

"Really?" I ask, tilting my head to the side.

"Really. I'm not much of a sharer outside these walls. I go on my trips to photograph amazing things, and I'm usually pretty solitary except for when I'm with a guide. And I don't make a habit of telling random strangers who I'm only going to be around for a few days or weeks my whole life story."

"That sounds like a pretty lonely existence," I murmur, watching her expression closely, but she's good at hiding what she's feeling.

"Nah, it's better for everyone if I don't get too close to anyone." Before I can ask what she means, she adds, "You're just the unlucky fucker who I've now chosen to be my bestie." She chuckles. "Isn't it funny how that works? One day, you just pick a human you've met, and you're like 'I like this one,' and then you do stuff with them. They become important to you just because you choose to let them be."

"Are you saying I'm important to you?" I prompt, the corner of my lips tilting up.

"Oh yes." She nods. "And that's why, after you get healed up enough to finish your deployment, and after I go back to the states, I'll be seeing you when you get home. No obligations. No relationship mumbo jumbo. Just a total understanding that you are now my best friend; you mean the world to me. You are the human I've picked to do stuff with."

She says it so matter-of-factly, like I have no say, and like her words aren't completely ridiculous according to the amount of time we've known each other. Clarice says she likes control, and with her last statement, I believe that. And for some odd reason, I also believe in what she said. She is now my best friend. She will be seeing me *when we're back in the US. All because she said so.*

And a small part of me recognizes that I really, really like believing in things just because she said so.

"So it was then you discovered you liked submitting to Clarice?" Doc asks.

"Not in the physical sense. That didn't come until later. But I liked the way she took the guessing out of everything else. She told me exactly what she wanted out of our friendship. It was clear we had the same aversion to a committed relationship albeit for different reasons," I reply.

"Your reason being the military, and hers being…?" he prompts.

"If I said I have a perfect understanding of her reasons, I would be lying. She's never come out and said 'This is why I do not want to be in a relationship…' But just from picking up on the different times she's always changed subjects and microexpressions, it's gotta be because of a past relationship. Which is strictly forbidden from being discussed."

"How does that make you feel?" he asks in his therapist's voice before adding, "You said there were no secrets between the two of you, yet this is something she won't talk to you about."

I nod. "It used to irk me that she wouldn't open up about that, but with time, I learned to embrace it. Because the closer I became to her, the more I realized I wouldn't like thinking about her with other men. I'd rather not know details of the other people she's given herself to. For the past eleven years, they've been faceless bodies. She's shared her sexual experiences with me through *showing* me her knowledge with physical acts. So I don't see them as secrets. I see it as a time in her life that doesn't exist anymore."

He thinks for a moment, looking at me closely, but I don't fidget. I have nothing to hide. I've been completely honest speaking about the way I feel.

"There is something in Clarice's past that is the reason she prefers being in a Dominant position sexually. In order for her to come as your guest to our club, you do understand I'm going to have to discuss those things with her, correct?"

"And I said before, good luck on that," I snort.

"But if she isn't willing to speak about them, she won't be allowed to come," he tells me.

"I'm aware, Doc. I'm hoping she gives you just enough tidbits of information that you can use your genius psychology brain to piece together why she is the way she is, and hopefully, it'll be good enough to get her in," I confide, scrubbing my hands down my face. "But she's a fucking vault."

"To you."

"Thanks for rubbing it in, dick," I grumble.

"You allow her to be. You don't want her to run, so you never press. Also, it's part of your Dominant/submissive relationship. It's her hard limit, and you respect that."

I press my lips together, nodding in agreement. "Putting it like that, yeah."

"But here's the thing. I'm not in a D/s relationship with her. I can press because I'm not scared of making her run. And from what you've told me about the time you spent with her overseas, and the fact that you've stayed close all these years, I don't think you'll have anything to worry about," he assures.

"I hope you're right."

"I'm always right." He smiles, and I can't help but chuckle.

"Well, my next appointment should be here by now. But I know we have a lot more to talk about. How would you feel about doing some sessions together with Clarice? I'll assess whether she's opening up enough while you're present, and if I think I can get more out of her with you not here, then we'll do that."

"What, like couples counseling?" I ask, furrowing my brow.

"Exactly like couples counseling. I believe that if Clarice sees how open and honest you are with your answers, it will inspire her to do the same."

I nod, my knee bouncing a couple times with anxiousness. "Good idea, Doc."

"I tend to have those quite often," he states, standing and placing his notepad on his side table.

"Yeah, yeah. I gotta get home. She'll be here in less than an hour," I tell him, and saying it out loud makes my heart thud.

"Sounds good. I'll see what I have free tomorrow and let you know what time to bring her," he says, clapping me noisily on the back before opening his office door to let me out and to welcome the man sitting on the couch in the waiting room.

I hurry out to my truck, ready to make some final touches to my house to make sure it's absolutely perfect for Clarice's arrival.

Chapter 7

Clarice

"Turn right in three hundred feet. Your destination will be on your left," the GPS tells me, and my stomach fills with a monsoon of excitement. I follow the directions, and sure enough, there's Brian's SUV parked in his long driveway.

The neighborhood itself is lovely, full of huge trees with lots of acreage between the houses. There isn't any grassy lawn space, so it feels like an entire community of homes scattered throughout the woods. I absolutely love it.

I pull in behind his truck and hop out. I'll grab my bags later, too anxious to see Brian. The house is gorgeous, and so very him. It's all dark wood, stone, and glass. The home is split in two with one room connecting the two parts. I can see into the left structure, because the front is entirely made of windows. It's a one-story space with high ceilings made of raw wooden beams.

chimney snuggles up to the right of it, and I can't wait to see what it looks like from the inside. The right half of the home is two stories, with an adorable porch on the bottom and a balcony to die for on the top. The right half of the house is much taller than the left, allowing the second floor to have the same vaulted ceilings as the left. Another chimney is butted up to this structure, and it makes me wonder which rooms those fireplaces are attached to.

Going to the front door, which has to be eight feet tall, I admire the dark wood framed by two huge windows. I barely have time to peek into the center one-story foyer before the door swings open, and there he is. The most beautiful man I've ever had the pleasure to be in the presence of. And I'm lucky enough to call him my best friend.

"Can I help you?" he asks, keeping a straight face.

I play along. "I seemed to have lost my way in the woods. I'm sorry to bother you, but I think I heard something lurking behind me, and I'm afraid it might be a big, bad wolf." I widen my eyes and jut my bottom lip out in a pout.

He smirks. "Well come inside, little one. I'll keep you safe."

I smile and step up to him, standing on my toes to wrap my arms around his neck, and his long, muscular arms immediately curl around my lower back to lift me higher against him. I breathe him in, realizing the woodsy scent I've always smelled on him wasn't artificial and from a bottle. No, it's the smell of his home. And just as I feared, it makes me fall in love with the place instantly.

"God, I've missed you," he murmurs into my hair.

My body goes completely lax against him, and I let him hold me up. "Missed you more," I confide, not blowing off the seriousness of his tone, because I've really… like *really* missed him this past month. No matter how busy I was with photography gigs and editing and everything else going on in my day-to-day life, he was never gone from my thoughts. I could never concentrate fully on what I was doing, because there he was, always whispering across my mind, the memories of all the time we spent together on his missions taunting me with their happiness.

He slowly lets me down, and then I quickly kick off my sandals, shaking off the heavy mood and doing a twirl in front of him as I grin up into his handsome face. "Show me around, big guy. This place is amazing!"

He looks almost relieved before his face splits into a wide grin as he takes my hand, leading me left toward the one-story side. Everything is all open, flowing seamlessly. The kitchen is one long line of marble, stainless steel appliances, and cabinetry along the wall, with an island of matching marble that stretches the same length, and as I look to the left, in front of the windows I had seen from the driveway, is the dining area and fireplace.

When my eyes twinkle up into his, he points up, and I let my head fall back to take in the swoon-worthy ceiling. The beams are even more breathtaking from directly beneath them, the height of the space astounding.

"You definitely found a place tall enough for you, big guy," I remark with a smile.

He chuckles. "Yeah, it was number one on my list of must-haves. The previous owner was a seven-foot-tall basketball player for the Tar Heels."

I laugh. "Fitting."

Next, he leads me to the other side of the home, which I see is the living area. It's filled with huge overstuffed couches and chairs with ottomans, and I let go of his hand to go to the fireplace. It's astonishing in all its stone and wooden mantel glory. If my camera weren't out in the car, I'd definitely snap a picture of it to drool over later.

I turn toward the set of stairs, admiring the banister that matches the same black metal holding the wooden beams of the ceiling in place, loving the way everything coordinates so flawlessly, as I make my way to the bottom step. I glance over my shoulder when I don't hear Brian's footsteps behind me, and I smirk when I see he's frozen in place, watching my ass as I walk away.

"Ya coming?" I ask, shaking my head with a giggle.

"Trying not to," he replies, and I glance down to see the outline of his thick cock through his jeans. God, it never gets old knowing how easily I affect him. "You just had to go with your sexy rocker girl look today, didn't you?"

"Um, three-hour car ride. You know good and well that translates to a three-hour concert featuring yours truly. Plus, the leggings and band tee are super comfy for driving." I shrug. I may be tone-deaf, but there's nothing I love more than singing to the radio at the top of my lungs. And it makes Brian laugh every time I ride with him, which makes it even better.

It's his turn to shake his head. "It should be illegal for an ass like that to go walking around in leggings," he says, finally making his way over to me and giving my right ass cheek a firm squeeze.

I swat at his hand, turning to trot up the stairs. At the landing, I see there are four doors up here. Opening the first door, I peek inside and see it's a bedroom. It's cozy but impersonal, none of Brian's clothes and things around the room, so I assume it's a guest room. I close it and move to the next, which is a beautiful but empty bathroom.

"You don't have company often, I take it?" My voice echoes in the hollow space, which doesn't even have towels to absorb my words.

"My parents come every once in a while. But if any of the guys come over, they normally just use the half-bath downstairs off the living room," he explains.

I nod, closing the door and moving to the next, which is a linen closet. It's stacked neatly with giant bath sheets, which I know he prefers over regular towels because of his larger-than-life frame. On the bottom shelf are extra sets of sheets, and I lift a brow, thinking to myself, *We'll probably need those later.*

Coming to the last door, which is far off from the rest, it's already open, as if inviting me inside. And the view takes my breath away. The back wall, which is actually the front of the house, is all glass, but it must be tinted, as the bedroom is lit and all I see is the reflection of the room with the faint outline of trees through the windows. The vaulted ceilings are just like the ones down in the kitchen and dining area, but it's the massive California king-size bed in the center that makes my heart sing. Framed by an ornately carved post in each corner, the bed is covered in the thickest, fluffiest white comforter and pillows I've ever seen, and it takes everything in me not to dive into them to see if they feel as heavenly as they look.

The rest of his furniture is as fit for a king as the bed is. Instead of a dresser, he has a tall chest of drawers in the same wood and style as the bedposts. There's a nightstand on each side of the bed, with a lamp on only the left side, which I know is Brian's preferred side to sleep on since I've spent countless nights snuggled up against him. Finally, there's a massive Armoire, its top cabinet doors open to reveal a flat-screen TV and various electronics.

"Check out the bathroom," Brian says, pointing toward a door off to the side.

When I flip on the switch, I actually have to take a step back to take it all in, my body coming flush up against his front. He wraps his hand around my hip, holding me steady as I make sounds ranging from squeaks to moans at the beauty before me. Marble, tile, and countertops. A glass-enclosed shower that could fit an army. A garden tub the size of a motherfucking Jacuzzi.

Ship. Lap. *Everything.*

Well, not everything, but the walls are lined with it, looking classy and welcoming at the same time. There's a closed door I assume has a toilet behind it, since there's not one in sight, and next to it is the open door to his closet, which I see is giant but mostly empty. On the outside of it, between the closet and the glass shower, is a throne. And not the kind one usually refers to when talking about a bathroom. It's the only way I can think to describe it. The gargantuan white armchair looks like it would belong to the same king who owns the furniture out in the bedroom, and as I glance into the mirror, seeing Brian is watching my reaction in our reflection, I smile gently, knowing it does.

This is Brian's castle, and I couldn't love it more.

I sashay over to the chair, spin, and fall into its depths, letting the velvety softness surround me. "Did you pick this yourself?" I ask curiously, running my hand over the arms and dipping my fingers into the divots where the grommets pull in the upholstery.

He watches my fingers, licking his bottom lip as I swirl them around the line of shallow holes. He clears his throat, meeting my eyes. "Uh, yeah. I, uh… I needed somewhere to sit and put on my shoes. The space was too large and looked silly with just the little stool I originally had there, so I got the biggest chair I could find."

"I love it," I say simply, and you'd think I just told him I saved his puppy from drowning if the look of relief on his ruggedly handsome face was anything to go by.

And it's then I realize… he must've been worried, worried over what I would think of his home. Here I was, fretting about falling even more in love with him to the point I wouldn't be able to leave, and my sweet Brian was obviously terrified over the thought I wouldn't like his place. The realization makes me feel like a bitch and a queen at the same time. I hate the fact that I'm closed off enough to make him worry that anything he owned wouldn't be absolutely perfect just because it was *his*. He could live in a one-room cabin with no running water, and it would be glorious just because it was *his* personal space. I wish I could show him how much he means to me, how much I love him, so he wouldn't have to stress about such things. But the fact that he does stress about whether or not I'd like something means everything in the world to me. My opinion matters to him. Him. Brian Glover. In my eyes, the world's greatest hero, since I've gotten to see him in action countless times. Not only that first time in Afghanistan, when he helped save his fellow soldiers, but also since he became a mercenary—a vigilante for the victims of unimaginable crimes. It astounds me just to think about such a man worrying about what I might think.

"You gotta stop looking at me like that, lover," comes his deep growl. "The whole rocker girl thing, dressed in all black, sitting like that in my big white chair, *in my house*… it's doing something to me." He adjusts his erection, and I lift a brow. "Just had to pick Metallica today, didn't you?"

I smile at that. He knows I have an obsession with graphic T-shirts, band tees being my favorite. "I was going to go with my Thirty Seconds to Mars one, but it was dirty."

He shakes his head. "Don't think that one would've had the same effect. Go with that one next time so I don't have to take you to dinner with blue balls."

"Mmm… dinner," I murmur, but my mouth is watering for a completely different reason. Dinner can wait. "Be a good host and come here."

He doesn't even blink. In two strides of his impossibly long legs, he stands before me, looming over me with his eyes alight with his obedience.

Feeling a sense of power, not only from his submission but from my position in this throne-like chair, I point to the floor at my feet. "On your knees," I order, my heart pounding as he follows my command. The position brings us face-to-face, and I can't help but to lean forward and kiss him tenderly. But only for a moment. I can't get lost in the feel of his love pouring from his lips. I have to focus on bringing us both pleasure through my domination. "If my clothes are bothering you so badly, you should take them off."

"Yes, ma'am," he drawls, and he reaches for my waistband first, effortlessly lifting my ass from the seat to pull my leggings off in one swift move that leaves me bare from the hips down. Pausing for a moment with his hands gripping the hem of my shirt, he bites his lip then meets my eye. "Metallica or titties… Metallica or titties…" he murmurs, and I squint at him.

"You better be joking or you'll be taking me to dinner with more than just blue balls. I'll slap a chastity device on your ass so fast you—"

"Titties it is," he cuts me off, pulling my shirt over my head and burying his face between my breasts. The swift change from the cold air to his heated touch sends a wave of goose bumps over my skin, hardening my nipples. What he's doing with his mouth along my flesh feels so good I lay my head back against the chair, letting him have his way while I take in every sensation.

I bury both hands in his hair, smiling at the fact that I know he's grown it out just because I like it. Gripping the light brown strands, I guide him lower, down my stomach, allowing him to spend a moment dipping his tongue into my navel before nipping at my soft belly. I haven't had abs in God only knows how many years, but it seems as my curves grew, so did his infatuation with my body, so I put aside any type of self-consciousness I might've had and embraced the fact his opinion was the only one that mattered to me.

His big hands grip my thighs. I can feel his fingers flexing and releasing, his pleasure in the feel of me there apparent in the catch of his breath. And the knowledge that I can affect this incredible man with just the touch of my skin against his causes liquid heat to coat my pussy.

Unwilling to hold out any longer, and knowing full well he's allowing me to do it since there's no way on earth I would be able to make him budge if he really didn't want to, I push him down until—

"*Fuuuck*," he growls against my core, the vibration making me suck in a breath. "So wet."

I've been so busy the last few weeks I haven't even used one of my solo toys, so the swipe of his tongue up my slit and around the bundle of nerves makes my legs convulse around his wide shoulders. I hold him to me, instinct taking over as my hips circle against his short beard.

"Oh, God," I moan, feeling the tendrils of my orgasm beginning to wrap around my center. And within seconds, as he sucks my clit between his lips, those tendrils squeeze with all their might, making me implode. My cry of pleasure echoes off the marble of the bathroom, and before the throbbing has a chance to wane, I push him back and stand on weak legs, pointing to the chair and ordering him, "Sit down."

When he does, I unbutton his jeans, grasp hold of them and his boxer briefs beneath, and pull them down his thighs, leaving them just below his knees as I straddle him and sink down on his rock-hard shaft. We both let out a sigh as he fills me to the brim, and with my pussy still coated in the wetness from his mouth and my desire, I begin to ride him with ease, even as he stretches me nearly to the point of pain.

The chair is the perfect firmness that it's little work to lift up and rock on my knees as I grip the back of his thick hair, pulling his head up from where he's watching my breasts bounce so I can kiss him.

"Oh, fuck," he groans, his eyes closing in concentration as I grind against him.

"I'm ready again, big guy. You can come when you're there," I allow, and his beautiful blue-green eyes open to meet mine, his brow furrowed as he clearly holds back from saying aloud what his face can't hide—he loves the fuck out of me.

And with that thought, I throw back my head and moan as a come, my pussy milking his cock until he grunts once, folding forward to bury his face in my neck as his orgasm hits him hard. His fingers dig into the muscles of my ass, rocking me a few more times until he finally melts back into the chair. It doesn't feel so big with his huge muscular body filling its depths.

I allow myself to collapse onto him, our panting breaths eventually evening out as we slowly come down from our high. I turn my face into his chest, breathing him in, and then sit up to smile into his. "Ya fed one set of lips, Bri. Time to feed the other," I tell him, and he lets out a bark of laughter.

"You're insatiable." He shakes his head, kissing me softly before taking hold of my hips and lifting me off him.

"Truth," I agree, walking naked to the door I figured hid the toilet and opening it. Seeing I was right, I close myself inside and clean up, noticing he bought the wet wipes I prefer. When I come out, I look at him, my eyes soft. "Did you buy those wipes for me?"

He shrugs. "Actually, I've been buying them for myself ever since I jacked some of yours when you brought them to one of the hotels we stayed at. My ass has never been so fresh."

I lift a brow. "Oh yeah? Should I add that to the list of things to test your limits on?"

"Fuuuck no," he drawls, standing and buttoning his jeans, tugging his shirt back into place. "I let you try that shit *one time*. Never again." He shakes his head.

"You gonna wash your face before we leave?" I ask, washing my hands in one of the two marble sinks in the counter.

"Of course not. This bad boy is my flavor saver," he says, his voice low and husky as he swipes a hand over his beard to smooth out the hairs that had been ruffled when he went down on me.

I can only sigh, knowing damn well he's serious. "You're so strange."

"But you like it," he says, swatting me on the ass before washing his own hands in the other sink, our eyes meeting in the mirror as he smiles.

This feels so normal, so natural, cleaning up together in his bathroom, as if this sink is actually mine and we do this every morning before work, like a real couple.

"So where do you feel like eating?" he asks me.

"McDonald's," I reply decisively. I'm not one of those girls who can't decide what they want to eat. When I'm hungry, it's usually for a certain type of food, and I don't talk myself out of it. The cravings just determine how many barre classes I do that week.

He shakes his head at me. "You come all this way to visit me, and you want me to take you to McDonald's?"

I turn my body to face him, propping my hip against the vanity as I dry my hands with a towel. "I'm a simple girl, Bri. And this simple girl needs her Mickey D's."

He chuckles. "As you wish."

Fifteen minutes later, we're at the front counter of the closest McDonald's.

"May I take your order?" the teenaged guy asks, his hands at the ready over his register.

Brian gestures to me. "Go ahead, babe."

Completely straight-faced, I tell him, "I'll have a McGangBang, please," and the teenager doesn't even bat an eye, putting it into his computer. After a long moment of total silence, waiting for Brian to order his dinner, I finally look over and up at him, and I fight with all my might not to burst out laughing at the look on his face. "What?"

He opens and closes his mouth a couple times, no words forming before he finally manages to speak. "Did you… just order something called a *McGangBang*?"

I lift a brow. "Um… yeah," I tell him in a *duh* voice.

He looks from me to the teenager then back again, confusion written all over his face. "Is that like… one of those secret menu items or something?"

The McDonald's employee takes the reins. "It's pretty popular. Even Lebron James orders it. You order the McDouble and the Spicy McChicken sandwiches off the dollar menu, take the bottom bun off one and the top bun off the other, and then you put them together."

"And voila, there you have the McGangBang. And it's fucking

delicious," I say with a grin.

And to my surprise, Brian turns to the boy, nods, and replies loudly, "I'll have *two* McGangBangs, please. And a large fry."

I run to the bathroom, almost peeing myself I laugh so hard.

Chapter 8

Brian

I don't think anything will ever top the feeling of Clarice sprawled on top of me, in *my* bed, in *my* home. When I wake up the next morning, after a night of just hanging out at my house before crawling into my bed with her, I realize it was the best night of sleep I've had in ages. Normally, I wake up several times a night to toss and turn until I finally lose consciousness out of pure exhaustion. On the nights I get to sleep next to her in hotel rooms, it's a little better, her presence soothing. But the combination of her beside me along with being in my own territory is priceless. I feel like a whole new man.

I run my hands up and down her back beneath my T-shirt she put on last night, and she groans unhappily into my chest, where I can feel a wet spot as her breath hits it. It makes me smile like an idiot.

"Uh-uh. Too early," she grumbles, as my hands rub her a little more insistently.

"Wakey, wakey," I singsong, feeling and hearing her suck in a bit to stop any more drool from escaping as she shakes her head.

"Why in God's name…," she whines, making me chuckle.

"We have our appointment with Doc in half an hour. I let you sleep as long as I could." I roll to my side, forcing her to roll to hers as I go, knowing full well she'd just lie on top of my other side if I don't. She's done it for as long as I can remember, sleeping right on top of me. I'd once told her I wanted to try one of those weighted blankets to see if it'd help me sleep at night, and she told me to save my money, sprawling her much smaller body across mine instead. Surprisingly, it worked, and she said she loved it too and that it reminded her of that scene in the first *Jurassic Park* when Alan lies on the Triceratops to feel it breathe.

"Ugggghhh," she groans, rolling to her back, and when I lean over her, as always, she slaps her hand over her mouth before I can kiss her. She fights her way out of the covers, her sexy tan legs kicking at the sheets before she stands and walks into the bathroom. I hear the sink turn on.

A minute or two later, she comes to stand next to the bed, her hair a nest on top of her head, her eyes a little puffy from sleep, her lips red from brushing her teeth, and a cranky look on her face.

She's never been sexier.

"What's the matter, grumpy gills?" I use the line she always quotes from *Finding Nemo*.

"What if he doesn't like me? What if he won't let me into the cool kids' club?" She pouts.

I sit up, scooting to the edge of the bed until she's standing between my legs. "The only way he's not going to let you in is if you don't answer his questions. Just be honest, and you'll be in like sin. And there's no way in hell he won't like you. Doc is the smartest guy I know, and he'd be stupid not to like you, lover," I tell her, rubbing my hands up and down her arms.

After a moment, she tucks her bottom lip back in and nods, straightening her shoulders. "Well, let's get this show on the road," she states, grasping the hem of my shirt she's wearing and whipping it off over her head. Before I can grab her naked body, she twirls then prances away, smirking as she grabs an outfit out of her suitcase. She slips on some flared blue jeans that fit her ass like a second skin, and a gray T-shirt with Luke's Diner across the back. She eyes me. "You gonna get dressed, big guy?"

I could sit here and watch her every movement for the rest of my life, but I shake myself out of the spell she put on me the second her breasts were exposed. I throw on some jeans and a black tee along with my usual boots, grabbing my keys off the top of my chest of drawers.

When we arrive at Doc's office, Clarice is a little hesitant to get out of the truck at first, but then she seems to give herself a little pep talk before reaching for the door handle. There's nervous energy radiating off her while we sit in the waiting room, and she jumps a little when his door clicks open.

Doc's smile is genuine when his eyes take us in, her hand held in mine as her toes make her flip-flop snap against her heel over and over where her legs are crossed. He gestures in welcome. "Brian, is this the lovely Clarice you've been telling me so much about?" he asks, and we stand.

"The one and only," I reply, my hand going to her lower back to urge her forward.

"It's so nice to meet you. Truly," Doc tells her quietly, holding out his hand to her. When she places her fingers against his palm, he engulfs her little hand with both his giant mitts, his expression emanating nothing but warmth. He's one of the only men I've met tall enough to look me in the eye, and instead of being intimidated, it's as if his size puts Clarice at ease, and I hope it's because it reminds her of me.

She relaxes into my side as Doc lets go of her hand. "Nice to finally meet you too, Doc. I feel like I already know you since Brian's been talking about you for years," she says, and we follow him inside the office before he shuts the door behind us. He gestures to the couch, and we take a seat.

"Well, I knew you existed, since it was through your amazing article about Brian that I found him. But I was admittedly very surprised to learn how important you've been to him these past eleven years," he explains, and I watch his ever-observant eyes take in the way she stiffens for a split second beside me.

She lets out a breath and then nods. "Yeah, he's pretty important to me too." She turns a small smile toward me before meeting Doc's gaze again. "The best friend a girl could ever ask for."

He picks up his notepad and pen from his side table, crossing his ankle over his opposite knee. "Has Brian explained how these sessions usually go?"

"Yes. I get to come and spill all my deepest, darkest secrets for the next four days in exchange for getting to go to your club." She turns to me. "And let me just say that if this club isn't as badass as you've described it to be, I'm kicking your ass."

I tell her out the side of my mouth, "Ninety-three different floggers split between five private rooms."

"Fuck me," she murmurs, sitting back on the couch and crossing her arms. "Where do we start, Doc?"

The two of us chuckle at her response, and Doc asks, "As curious as I am to ask you about how you were brought into the world of BDSM, it's better if we start at the beginning of your life and go in order, so we don't skip something that could be important."

Clarice nods, slipping off her flip-flops and pulling her legs up beneath her. I know Doc is taking in every little microexpression, every hint her body language gives off, in order to derive more from these sessions than what just her words provide. And with her arms crossed and her legs up, she's basically placed herself in the fetal position, unconsciously guarding herself as much as possible.

Doc knows exactly how to put her at ease. "I don't know how in-depth Brian has explained the purpose of these sessions, so I'll just give you a crash course." When she nods, he continues, "In order for our club to maintain the highest caliber of safety, we are very careful of who we allow membership. With the level of trust a submissive gives a Dom who will be using potentially dangerous equipment and devices during a scene, we have to make sure we aren't accepting anyone with ill intentions into what should be our haven. These sessions weed out a Dominant who might want to harm someone. We permit sadism, of course, but there's a difference between a person who wants to provide pain to a masochist who derives pleasure from it, and a person who wants to just hurt someone."

"That's brilliant. Really. I've been to so many clubs before where a Dominant has gone too far with their sub, not listening to their safewords and such," Clarice replies, and before I realize the sound is coming from me, a growl fills the room. She looks up at me and pats my thigh. "Not me, big guy. I only play sub for you."

"Play sub?" Doc prompts. "I'm aware we're going out of order here, but I can't help but ask." He glances between the two of us, and I reach up to rub the back of my neck.

"About that. We didn't get that far during our solo sessions for me to tell you, Doc." Heat radiates out of the collar of my T-shirt. But I promised I would be totally honest and open during our times with Doc in order to let Clarice know it was okay for her to be too. So I just let the words tumble out. "She and I are switches."

He lifts his brows but then nods. "Actually, that's not all that surprising. From the stories you've been telling me, it makes perfect sense."

"What have you told him?" Clarice cuts in, a small smile on her face.

"Well," Doc answers for me, "he explained that you're a bit older than he is—"

"Only five years," she murmurs defensively.

"—so, therefore, a bit more sexually experienced. He had only been with two partners before meeting you, and you were already well versed in BDSM by then. We hadn't made it to the first time the two of you had intercourse—"

"Ew. He really is a doctor, isn't he? *Intercourse*," she says in my direction with a shudder.

Doc seems like he can't help the chuckle that escapes him. He looks at me. "It's like a therapy session with Seth. Can you imagine a conversation between him and Clarice?"

"We'll never get a word in," I agree.

She bounces a little in her seat. "I totally can't wait to meet him. He's so funny on the phone. It's really hard to keep quiet and not laugh when Bri talks to him during his missions."

All I can do is shake my head.

"We've managed to go way off course now. My fault, I should've known better," Doc says, making a note on his pad of paper. "All right, Clarice. Let's start at the beginning. What can you tell me about your childhood?"

I feel her weight lean against my side, and I automatically wrap my arm around her, letting it rest on the back of the couch as she begins to speak.

"I actually had a pretty great childhood. My parents are super supportive of what I do. I'm an only child, and we did a lot of traveling my whole life. That's where I got my love of photography. They're flight attendants. During the school year, they only did domestic flights on alternating schedules. But during the summer, they flew internationally on the same routes, and they were able to take me with them. I considered myself pretty lucky that I was able to grow up in one place with parents who had severe cases of wanderlust." She smiles.

"From what I know about you, you come by the same wanderlust honestly," Doc acknowledges.

"Definitely. It would be miserable for me to be stuck somewhere for too long. That's why Brian's and my friendship is so awesome. He calls me up and is like, 'Hey, we're going to Nashville, or New York, or Florida,' just out of nowhere. I love it," she says, her voice enthusiastic.

He eyes her for a moment, reading deeper into her answer than what she's probably used to. "So there was nothing momentous that happened during your childhood that stands out to you? No deaths in the family, nothing traumatic."

She purses her lips, shaking her head slowly. "Not that I can think of."

"What about in your teenage years?" he presses.

"Nope, regular ole high school stuff. I wasn't popular, but I wasn't the lowest on the totem pole either. I had my small group of friends I hung out with all four years, and we were kind of just invisible. I wasn't bullied, or anything." She shrugs.

"Young adulthood?" he prompts.

"I went to college and studied photography. Very soon after I graduated, I was hired on to *Sands of Time Magazine* by someone who discovered my website when one of my photos of wildfires in California went viral. They sent me all over the world, including Afghanistan, where I met the big guy here." She hitches her thumb at me. "Oh, there's a traumatic experience for ya. I was like, twenty feet away from an IED that went off. That was pretty crazy."

Doc makes a note then lifts his head once more. "And finally, adulthood."

"Uuuumm… Oh! That serial killer in Raleigh tried to put me in his trunk. That was a little terrifying. But Brian saved the day. He tends to do that." She smiles over at me.

"Clarice," Doc calls, pulling her attention back to him. "You realize you never once mentioned a single relationship in all of your summaries?"

She shifts on the couch cushion. "I'm aware."

"And yet, from what I gathered from Brian, you were sexually experienced when you met him. Already versed in BDSM, in fact."

"I was," she murmurs, obviously not liking where this line of questioning was going.

Doc swipes a hand down his beard, thinking for a moment before he speaks. "I believe we're going to have to use a different tactic with your sessions."

"Oh?" Her voice sounds nervous.

"Most people, when we get to the teenage years, don't graze

over them so quickly without mentioning a single love interest. They at least talk about their first crush. And once we move on to the young adulthood, they have even more to say about the people who were in their lives. Not just their education and career. And once we get to adulthood, unless the person is a virgin—which would very rarely, practically never be the case—they wouldn't be attending these sessions in order to be granted access to a BDSM club. You obviously weren't a virgin when you met Brian. And you obviously practiced the lifestyle with someone before him. Yet you never once mentioned any one person of importance while you were talking," he points out.

I look between Doc and Clarice. This is the moment I've been dreading since all this began. He's pressing her, much further than I've ever tried since I've always been wary of pushing so hard that I'd drive her away. Instinctively, my arm tightens around her, as if to keep her from taking flight, hoping she'll choose to fight instead.

Her voice is quiet when she answers. "I've had one actual boyfriend in my life. And I had a friend who was a sub who introduced me to the world of BDSM. After that, I've had quite a few sexual partners, but no actual relationships."

"Can you expand on that, please?" he asks, his pen at the ready.

"Um… I'd rather not, if that's all right." She swallows. "That was so many years ago, and I've moved on."

Doc watches her closely, and I wonder if he can see the slight trembling of her body that I feel with her pressed against me. "There's nothing you'd like to add? The story of how you met your one boyfriend, maybe?"

"Mm, not really. He was just a boy. We had regular, vanilla sex. He never hurt me. And when I got into BDSM, no one hurt me there either. And for the last eleven years, I've only been with Brian," she states, and a sense of relief I didn't know I was holding out for washes over me.

All these years, we didn't talk about things like that. We made the agreement a long time ago that we would only sleep with each other without protection, with the promise that we would always use condoms if we slept with anyone else. I tried to put it out of my head that she might be having sex with other people, holding onto the trust that I was the only one who got to feel her bare, with nothing between us. And I certainly wasn't fucking anyone else. No one could possibly compare to Clarice, so what would be the point?

Doc then puts his notepad back on his side table, placing his pen on top of it, before leaning forward in his seat to rest his elbows on his knees, clasping his hands together. His eyes bore into Clarice's so intensely I feel like he's trying to look into her soul. When I glance at her, she's pale, and she looks more petrified than I've ever seen her.

That's when Doc drops a bomb, taking aim directly in the center of the fortress Clarice has built around herself.

"You've never been hurt. There's never been anyone in your life who's important enough to mention now. Yet when the one person you gush about, the one person you're holding onto for dear life—" He gestures to where she's now gripping my shirt at my side. "—tries to portray his love for you, you hold him at arm's length. If you've never been hurt, then why do you refuse to acknowledge the fact that you too are 100 percent completely in love with the man you call your best friend?"

And for the first time in all the years I've known Clarice Lorenson, she runs from me, her eyes welling with tears as she rushes out of the office, the door slamming behind her.

Chapter 9

Clarice

"Clarice, wait!" Brian calls behind me as I walk as fast as my legs will take me without actually breaking into an all-out run. I have no idea where I'm going. All I know is I need to get away from the two men who were in that room, and I need to do it now.

But I don't get far down the street before his much longer stride not only catches up to me, but passes me enough to where he's suddenly making like a wall for me to run right into. He doesn't embrace me. He doesn't try to trap me within his arms. And I'm grateful, because I'm scared I would show him a side of myself—an ugly, hysterical, irrevocable side of myself—that would leave me more than a little embarrassed if he saw me that way. Instead, we just stand here, my face buried in his chest, our arms at our sides as he allows me to just breathe him in.

I inhale through my nose, my exhales shuddering and painful as I try to rein my emotions back under control. I feel his pecs flexing, and I imagine he's using every bit of his self-control not to wrap himself around me, waiting for me to tell him what I need. Exactly what I've trained him to do.

I reach up and grasp one of his biceps in my hand before turning my head to the side to rest my ear against his heart. My eyes are tightly closed as I listen to the drum of his pulse, letting it calm me. He's still alive. He's still strong, healthy, and *alive*, all because I haven't allowed us to give in to our feelings for each other.

"I'm sorry, big guy," I whisper, and I realize I've tried to speak before I'm ready, because tears escape down my exposed cheek. My throat burns as I try to hold in a sob.

"You don't need to apologize, little one." His voice rumbles in his chest.

I shake my head against him. "I do, Bri. I thought I could go in there and just breeze right through this shit, but Doc…."

"Yeah. I know, babe. He's not your average therapist who just bullshits his way through the hour to collect the insurance money," he murmurs, finally placing his hand around the back of my neck and squeezing gently to massage the tension there.

"I'm so embarrassed," I admit, my face flushing. "How am I going to face him again after running out of there like a stupid, dramatic girl?"

His chuckle warms me from the inside out, but in a good way, unlike my humiliated blush. "I can assure you, you're definitely not the first, and you won't be the last. He's a tough fucker who will call you out without blinking, but he's been successful in healing even the most helpless of patients." He pauses a moment, and then tells me, "If you'd be more comfortable doing your sessions without me in there, I'll completely under—"

"No." I shake my head. "That's ridiculous. There's nothing I would tell another person that I wouldn't tell you. You know me better than anyone else ever has. If I have to talk to Doc, you're going to be there."

The thought of telling a stranger something I haven't been able to bring myself to tell Brian feels almost like… cheating. I know how outrageous that sounds, even to myself, but it's like that part in *The Kissing Booth*, when Elle asks herself, *If you wouldn't want your best friend to know what you're doing, should you be doing it at all?* He's my person, my conscience, everything that is good and right in my world. I know it's strange to think that about a man whose job it is to kill people. But those are terrible people who make this world a scary and bad place, and everyone—and I mean *everyone*—is better off without them here to wreak havoc.

But it's been a dream of mine for years to come see Brian's club. And now that I've met Doc and see that I won't be able to beat around the bush in our sessions, I'm up in the air about whether or not my dream is worth the possibility of losing Brian. If I were to tell them the truth, they'd laugh me off. They wouldn't take my fears seriously. And that, above everything, would hurt me more than anything in my past.

"I don't know if I can do this, Bri," I confess, and his heart begins to pound at my words and he stiffens. I look up into his eyes, seeing the worry there, and it occurs to me he might've taken it the wrong way. "The sessions, I mean. I don't know if I can dig up everything I've buried deep and tried to forget for much longer than I've even known you. You know me. You know I do my best not to look behind us and am always looking forward to our next adventure."

He lifts his hand to trace my jawline, sending a thrill down my neck and around my heart. "How about we come to tomorrow's session, and you decide then? Now that you've experienced one of Doc's appointments, maybe you'll be better prepared the next time."

I nod, seeing the hope in his eyes. "I can do that."

Several hours later, we're in Brian's truck, heading to Corbin and Vi's new house for dinner. I'm pretty nervous about seeing him again, since the first and only time I met him before had been that day in Afghanistan, and he hadn't been the nicest person toward me. Brian assures me he's a completely different person than the one I met, but first impressions and all that.

When we pull into the driveway of the pretty white two-story plantation style home, I see several people sitting on the wraparound front porch, and my heart begins to pick up its pace. These are Brian's people. These are the most important people in his life, the ones he sees every day, who he works with, trusts with his life, and the ones who have helped mold him into the person he is today. I have no idea what he's told them about me, or if we're showing up and I'll be a big surprise to everyone. All I know is he told me to throw on some clothes after we had the best shower sex in the history of ever in his massive shower as he described everything he'd imagined when I caught him fucking his fist in Afghanistan. Then he told me we were heading to Corbin's for a new weekly tradition that started about a month ago when his wife Vi demanded they all meet up on Friday nights for dinner before they went to work at the club.

"Do they know I'm coming?" I ask him when he reaches for

his door handle.

"I had a long talk with them the night before you got here. They're excited to meet you, lover," he promises, and I give him a nervous smile.

"All right. Let's do this," I say, and he hurries around the front of his truck to open my door.

"Awwww, he's being such a gentleman!" I hear a woman's voice coo from the porch, followed by a couple rounds of shushing.

"Oh hush," comes a different female voice. "I was thinking the same thing, Vi. And why don't you open my door for me like that?" she asks, and I pull my lips between my teeth to keep from laughing. Brian's always done that for me. He said his momma would kick his ass if he didn't open a door for a lady.

"There are no doors on a motorcycle, doll. Sheesh!" comes the reply.

Oh my gosh. That was Seth! He's the only one out of the guys who rides a motorcycle, as far as Brian's told me. And suddenly I'm completely giddy to meet everyone instead of anxious.

"Yeah, but we have *my* car." And that confirms it. That was totally Twyla.

Excitement gets the best of me, and I pick up my pace, forcing myself not to break into a run. When we reach the steps, everyone stands up from their rocking chairs to greet us except for the dark-haired woman who's currently holding a sleeping baby in her arms, but she beams the most beautiful smile at me when our eyes meet.

"She does exist!" The voice I recognize distinctly as Seth's comes from a handsome bearded man with laughing eyes. "Nice to meet you, Clarice," he tells me, holding out his hand. But I shove it to the side and wrap my arms around his neck, doing a happy little dance before pulling away.

"Oh my God! You're Seth! I feel like I already know you. I've heard so many conversations between you and the big guy on his missions. Thank you so much for all the shit you give him. Happy to know I'm not the only one," I ramble. "I'm serious. If I didn't have Bri, I'd totally make you my BFF."

"Hey! That's *my* bestie. I will fight you," the dark-haired woman holding the baby calls, and when I peek around Seth's shoulder, she grins and winks at me.

"Um, both you bitches need to back off. That's my *husband* you're fighting over," the beautiful woman next to Seth, with a cute black bob and thick-rimmed glasses, says with a chuckle. I glance down to see her rubbing her small baby bump and smile.

"Oh my gosh, Twyla. You're pregnant?" I choke out, my eyes getting misty. I look up at Brian. "You didn't tell me?"

"Don't look at me with those accusey eyes. I only found out this week. I got so busy with all the Doc sessions and preparing for your visit I totally forgot to tell you," he replies, tucking a piece of hair behind my ear.

"I guess that's acceptable," I grumble, turning back to Twyla. "Congratulations, you two. I'm so happy for you I could seriously cry. Brian's told me so much about all of you. I feel like I've been right here with y'all through everything."

A man covered in tattoos, wearing a black V-neck tee that shows off the top of his chest piece, steps up on the other side of Seth. "Which is surprising to hear, since none of us even knew you existed. Well… except me. I met you a long, long time ago. And I just wanted to say I'm sorry for how rude I was back then."

"Sgt. Lowe," I breathe, hardly able to speak. Because the man before me may favor the heartbroken person I met in Afghanistan, but now, he's practically glowing with happiness, and I know for certain Brian was right. I shake myself. "Corbin, I mean. Sorry. Oh gosh, I'm so happy you got your wife back. Oh, shit. Why am I so weepy?" I fan at my eyes.

He chuckles, and I barely contain my groan as he tries to lighten the mood by saying in a put-on creepy voice, "Hello, Clarice."

Before I can pretend to laugh, Seth cuts me off. "Ugggghhh, seriously?"

"What? *The Silence of the Lambs*. I thought you'd be impressed I actually used a movie quote," Corbin says, his brow furrowing at his friend.

"Maybe if you got the quote *right*, fucker." As if I didn't like Seth enough.... "Hannibal Lector never says 'Hello, Clarice' in *The Silence of the Lambs*."

"Bullshit. Everyone knows that line. Even people who haven't seen the mov—"

Seth shakes his head. "Negative, Ghost Rider. Dr. Lector tells the FBI trainee, 'Good evening, Clarice,' at one point, but after someone misquoted the line, everyone remembered it the wrong way. It was so popularly remembered incorrectly that they put 'Hello, Clarice' in the *sequel*. But it was never in the original classic. Google it if you don't believe me. It's called the Mandela Effect."

"Who needs Google when we have a literal genius on the payroll?" Corbin concedes.

"This is the first time in my life I wasn't the one who had to explain that shit." I grin at Seth, and I feel Brian's arm come around me before he pulls me into his side.

"Oooo, someone's getting a little possessive," Seth teases him. "Don't worry. I'm no longer Mr. Steal Ya Girl. Ouch!" He rubs at the spot on his chest Twyla just smacked. "What, doll? Geez! I said no longer!"

"Quit picking on Brian," she scolds at her husband. "This is a big deal for him."

Seth's face softens before turning his eyes to mine. "It really is great to meet you. Even though it's kinda fucked up we never knew about you." He narrows his pretty hazel eyes up at his best friend. "But I can see he wanted to keep you all to himself. I'd be nervous to introduce my girl to the awesomeness that is me too." At Twyla's light growl, he grins. "Kidding. Sorta."

"I'm Vi, by the way," I hear coming from behind everyone, and they part down the middle so I can see the woman in the rocking chair clearly. "I promise I'm not trying to be rude. This little guy was just too big to come out on his own three weeks ago, and I had to have a C-section. And Daddy still gets pissy when I try to walk around, even though I'm fine now." She squints at Corbin before blowing him a kiss.

I wiggle out of Brian's hold and make my way over to her, kneeling beside her. Without disturbing the sleeping little angel in her arms, I squeeze Vi's bicep, smiling up at her. "I know you don't know me yet, but I'm so, so happy for you. Thank you for being one of Brian's first friends when he joined the army and got stationed here. Who knows what he would've been like when I met him in Afghanistan if you and Corbin hadn't pulled him out of his funk with rock climbing?"

Her eyes alight with surprise and then warmth. "Man, he really has told you every little detail about all of us, huh?" At my nod, she continues, "Which totally explains why he's such a grump all the time."

I tilt my head to the side in question. "A grump? Brian?" I glance over at him, my brows furrowed. "He's the sweetest and happiest person I know. I've only seen him grumpy a handful of times in more than a decade."

A hush falls over the group, and I look around, confused at all their shocked faces.

It's Seth who breaks the silence first. He bursts out with contagious laughter that spreads across the rest of the friends. Except for Brian. He crosses his arms over his chest and raises his brow at me. I can't help but giggle.

"Obviously, he saves all his happy energy for you, Clarice," Vi says. "When he's home and not on a mission, he's like a lost—"

"All right, guys. Shall we head inside? I'm starving," Brian interrupts her, taking a step toward me.

I stand but lean down to her ear before he pulls me away. "We can talk later," I stage-whisper so he can hear.

"Not gonna happen, lover," he grumbles before asking the group, "Is Doc coming?"

Twyla replies, "Yeah, he had a late appointment and then was swinging by his house to pick up my sister."

"Ah, fuck," comes out of my mouth before I can stop it, and all eyes turn to me as my cheeks grow warm. "Uh, sorry. My session didn't go too well with him earlier. It didn't even dawn on me I'd have to face him tonight after running out of his office."

"Oh, please, girl," Vi starts. "I've stormed out a few times. He's freaking psychic, or clairvoyant, or whatever the hell it is where he can read your mind. But I promise he doesn't take it personally and he won't hold it against you."

I relax tremendously. I'd been worried about the next time I'd see Doc again, if I'd be scolded for cutting our session short.

"When we go inside, be careful not to let the door slam. If we wake Genevieve up and she hears Seth's voice, she'll never go back to sleep. We'll be eating dinner out on the back patio tonight.

Corbin is grilling chicken and beef for fajitas," Vi tells us.

"Yeah, Seth. So keep your loud ass quiet," Corbin adds.

Seth smirks. "Don't be jelly your toddler loves me more than you."

"She doesn't love you more. She just identifies more with your maturity level," Corbin taunts, and Seth sticks his tongue out at him, making me laugh. But we all shut up as soon as Brian reaches for the screen door handle, unwilling to face Vi's wrath.

We make it to the kitchen without being too loud, and I follow everyone's lead when they get their own drinks out of the refrigerator before going out the back door to the patio there. It's as if the wraparound porch has been stretched out several yards, fitting a badass outdoor kitchen with a huge round table large enough to fit all of us and then some.

"You think he'll ever let me climb the damn stairs again, or will I be forced to live on the first floor until he can carry me up at night for the rest of my life?" Vi grumbles as she steps through the back door, her arm hooked through Seth's. She walks slowly and slightly hunched forward, and it makes my own womb ache watching her.

"You're technically not supposed to be carrying the baby around anyway for like, three more weeks, sweet cheeks. Give yourself time to heal. Corbin is just trying to take care of his most prized possessions. Think of it as his way of making up for lost time. You know he still feels guilty for that shit," he tells her softly.

She sighs. "It's been three years since we got back together. He doesn't need to feel guilty anymore."

"Babe, he'll feel guilty for missing out on that decade for the rest of his life. Just let him dote on you. Enjoy it. You deserve it. You just birthed two whole humans in as many years. Let it happen."

I love seeing their friendship. If it wasn't my first time meeting everyone, I would snap photos of these precious moments, but they'd probably find it weird since they don't know me the way I feel like I know them already.

Corbin exits a couple minutes later, and he comes over to where Vi is seated at the round table three seats to the right of me and hands her a baby monitor, kissing her forehead before making his way over to the grill. I assume he'll sit next to her in the empty seat to her left, as Brian slides out the one next to it before wrapping his arm around the back of my chair. On the other side of Vi is Seth, then Twyla.

I look up just as a stunning blonde walks through the back door, singsonging a hello to everyone as she heads straight for the seat next to Twyla. This must be her sister, as the blonde kisses her on the cheek before leaning over and kissing her belly.

Twyla giggles. "Is this the greeting I get to look forward to for the next five months, Auntie Astrid?"

"I gotta make sure she comes out knowing who her favorite aunt is. When it was just the two of us growing up, I didn't have any competition. Now I've gotta beat out this bitch." She gestures to Vi with a playful smile and then spots me. "Oh hell. Not another one. I'm gonna have to up my game."

I choke out a laugh. "Nice to meet you too. You must be Astrid," I tell her, and she gives me a genuine smile.

"And judging by the way Brian looks as if he's finally extracted the stick that's perpetual betwixt his buttocks, you must be Clarice. You have no idea how excited Neil was when he came home from work the other day after Brian told him about you," Astrid confides.

"Neil?" I look between her and Brian, but before either of them can answer, Doc takes the seat next to her, which puts him right next to me, completing the circle.

"That would be me," he clarifies, and I gulp before looking away.

Well, shit. Vi had made me feel much better when she told me she's ran out on appointments before, but now that he's here, the embarrassment of my dramatics overwhelms me.

But before I can completely fold in on myself to the point I'd be a ball in Brian's lap soon, Doc reaches over and pulls my hand off my can of Dr. Pepper, holding it between both of his. I look up at him, startled.

"You are an intelligent, remarkably talented, lovely woman, and I am honored that you are instilling your trust in me enough to try another session tomorrow," he says gently, and all I can do is nod, my mouth slightly agape. Even more quietly, so only Brian and I can hear, he tells me, "There is pain buried deep inside you that you've done a brilliant job of moving forward from, but it may be affecting you more than you believe. If you allow me to help you, the life you so enjoy now won't even be a blip on the radar of how good it *could* be."

In my mind, I go back to all the stories Brian has told me about Doc. He's helped heal women who've gone through far worse experiences than I ever have, so I totally believe he could do what he promises. But no matter how much of a magician on the disturbed psyche he might be, not even he could break what feels like a curse that's been placed on me since I was ten.

"I'll try my best," I murmur, and he gives my hand a squeeze before letting me go. When I look around the table, only Astrid is watching our exchange. If anything, I would expect a look of possessiveness, seeing how Brian told me she and Doc have this complicated thing going on between them. But that's not what I see in her pretty blue eyes. It's sympathy, like she wants to say something reassuring but doesn't want to embarrass me in front of everyone. I give her a small smile before turning to look up at Brian, who leans down to place a swift kiss to my lips. It surprises me just as much as Doc holding my hand, if not more. The fact that he'd kiss me in front of all the important people in his life makes me feel warmer than I've ever felt in my life. Sweltering, even. But in a very, very good way.

The rest of the evening goes amazingly. Seth makes us laugh until we can't breathe. Corbin and Vi tell me stories of Brian from before I met him. Doc and Astrid are entertaining to watch—her obviously fighting her attraction to him, while he looks about ready to throw her over his shoulder and haul her away. And Twyla, sweet, quiet Twyla, fills us in on all the coolest new toys that just arrived at the novelty story she works for, Toys for Twats.

I can see exactly why Brian describes them as his brothers, his family. And if I had one wish, one dream I dared to put out in the universe, it would be to become a permanent part of this circle, not just as a visiting friend, but as a member of their traditions.

It's in this moment I decide, for better or worse, I will confess my darkest secrets.

Chapter 10

Clarice

"I need to preface this session before we begin," I say into the quiet room. I sit, perched on the very edge of the leather sofa in Doc's office. My body feels like it wants to take flight all on its own, but my heart knows what I need to do. It's time, way past time I tell Brian the one last jigsaw piece that makes up the puzzle that is me. It's the one piece he's somehow been able to ignore, allowing the rest of me to be displayed for his appreciation, his eyes skimming over that one blank spot that would show him the whole picture. It's up to him to decide whether or not if, once the puzzle is complete, he wants to tear it all apart and throw it away, or if he'd like to frame it, preserving it as a treasure to keep for years to come.

"Of course," Doc replies. "Say whatever you need."

I nod, trying to decide where to begin. Brian is a statue beside me. It's as if he's afraid to move, worried I'll run away again. I hate to be the reason he's in any way uncomfortable, so I reach over and take hold of his hand, for both his reassurance and to help anchor me.

"What I'm about to tell you, you're not going to believe me. You're going to want to laugh it off. You're going to want to wave it away and tell me it's all in my head, that I have nothing to worry about, that I'm silly for letting this fear rule my life," I state, staring at the notepad resting on Doc's leg that's crossed over the other. For some reason, I can't meet either of their eyes. If I'm exposing this much of myself, I at least want to hide my soul. They won't be able to break my heart if they're unable to see my soul.

"I've never and will never discourage anything you have to say, lover. Especially something you've held onto so tightly all these years," Brian promises.

"I'm just saying… if I were to spill my guts in here, and y'all were to blow it off, that would pretty much devastate me. Because this secret I've held onto for so long, I've only done it to protect you." My eyes turn to meet his for a split second, just long enough to let him see the unshed tears that suddenly sprung there so he knows how serious this is to me. His fingers tighten between mine, letting me know he understands.

"And I'd like it stated that nothing is ever just in one's head. Every thought is created by an external factor, no matter how small it might be. I'm aware we've just met and you don't know me very well, but I'm not one to overlook even minor details. Whatever you have to say, I will take you seriously, Clarice," Doc assures.

I nod, finally scooting back in the couch. Brian must sense I need my space because he lets me tug my hand free and doesn't try to hold me. I pull my legs up to sit Indian style, my hands resting in my lap.

"Okay, well. You wanted me to start with my childhood. It was exactly as I said, completely wonderful. And then I made a friend when I was ten. His name was Kasey, and he was nicer than any boy I'd ever met before. He shared his lunch with me, because his mom baked him the best cookies, and we always sat next to each other, because we liked to read the same books." I look down and start toying with my anklet. "One day, Kasey slipped me a note, the typical one of that age, a multiple-choice question asking if I'd be his girlfriend, yes or no." I can't help but smile. The innocence of it all chokes me up. "Of course I checked yes. Who better to be your boyfriend than the nicest kid in your class? He shared his cookies, after all." I look up at Brian. "And you know cookies are my weakness, even back then."

He gives me a small smile and nod, knowing I'm rambling because I'm nervous. "Chocolate and pecan is your favorite," he murmurs.

I grin. "They're the best," I reply, and then turn back to my anklet. "The following week, Kasey didn't come to school. I was really worried, because he never, ever missed school. He always got to go up on stage and receive the perfect attendance award. And then the next week, he was gone too. Then, our teacher had us all turn our desks so we were sitting in a circle, and she told us Kasey had gotten really ill. At the time, she explained his lungs were sick, and when I was older I understood he had pneumonia." A tear slowly makes its way down my cheek, and I bat it away like an annoying fly. My eyes finally meet Doc's. "Kasey passed away the next day."

"I'm sor—"

"Teenage years was next, wasn't it? Or something like that," I interrupt Brian, not wanting to veer off the path. I need to get it all out at once. "When I was a sophomore in high school, I had a huge crush on a junior named Nicholas. He was just the right mix of nerdy and cool. We had a few classes together, and we had this really easy friendship. It's like, when we met, a part of us already knew each other, so there really wasn't a distinct getting-to-know-you stage." I smile over at Brian again. "You know how I like to just jump into friendship with both feet."

He reaches out and swipes a wayward tear from my nose, his face soft. He doesn't say anything this time, prompting me to continue.

"When homecoming came around, I was completely shocked when he asked me to go with him. I mean, we were good friends and I had a crush on him, but I had no idea he felt strongly enough about me that he'd want to take me as his date. Obviously, I immediately said yes." I let out one yelp of laughter that sounds more pained than joyful. "The night before homecoming, there was a party." I feel Brian stiffen next to me, but I don't look over at him, focusing all my attention on the tiny rifle charm on my anklet he'd given me years ago. "Nicholas invited me to go, but my flight attendant mom was finally home from doing a three-day trip and we had a girl date planned. We were getting our nails done, face masks, all that stuff chicks do in preparation for a big date the next day."

I clear my throat, leaning my head against the back of the couch to stare at the ceiling, trying to keep the tears from falling out of my eyes. "Nicholas wasn't in class the next morning."

"Oh, fuck," Brian whispers beside me, and he reaches over to squeeze my knee before letting me be.

"Oh, fuck is right, big guy," I mumble. "It turned out everyone had taunted Nick into doing a couple keg stands when they found out he'd never done one before." I sigh, lifting my arms to press the heels of my palms into my eye sockets. He flipped his car on the way home after veering off the road and losing control. He died at the hospital that night."

I sit back up, looking at Doc. "What was it, young adulthood next?"

He nods solemnly. "That's right, Clarice."

"By now, I was thinking it was just a coincidence, right? The only two boys who asked me out died just a few weeks after I said yes?" I gesture between Brian and Doc, and they give me a nod to pacify me. "Enter Zachary Mitchel. He was so freaking hot, lemme tell you. He was my first *real* boyfriend. I met him the summer after I graduated high school. He was going into the army, and I was starting my first semester of college that fall when I finally gave up my V-card."

I shift on the couch again, spinning to lie down and put my head on the armrest while tucking my toes under Brian's thigh, my knees pointing to the ceiling. I cross my arms, suddenly feeling cold. "He was great. We saw each other often before he went to boot camp, and then he was stationed at the base not far from my school. It was like fate was lining everything up for us to be together. We dated for nearly two years before he was deployed. And the night before he got on that plane, he asked me to marry him."

Brian jerks his face toward me, and I glance over my knees to see his shocked eyes.

"I said yes, and the next day, I gave him the last kiss I'd ever give him. He was killed in action three weeks later." My face crumples then, and the tears stream into my hairline at my temples. I cover my face with my hands, letting out a sob.

Before I know what's happening, I'm in Brian's lap, his big body surrounding me in a cocoon of warmth. My face presses into his throat as I cry like I've never allowed myself to cry before, my body jerking with the emotion pouring out me, as my best friend in the world tries to keep me together. One of his arms leaves me for a moment, and when he wipes my nose, I realize Doc must've been handing him tissues.

"That's why," Brian says to the top of my head, running his huge palm up and down my back. "That's why you never let me tell you how much I love you." I gasp sharply at the ease in which he confesses how he feels about me, and I reach up to fist the front of his shirt, holding on to him for dear life. "Because you know after telling you that, I'd ask you to be with me. And you're scared, since every other man you've ever said yes to has died, that it'd happen to me too."

"Yes," I wail, the agonized sound breaking off into sobs as I press into his body as close as I can without actually becoming a part of him.

"Clarice—"

"Please don't, Bri. Please don't just say 'That won't happen to me,'" I beg, lowering my voice in a weak attempt at mimicking his. "Because that's exactly what Zack said when I told him about Kasey and Nicholas and why I had never had a real boyfriend before. And then he died too. They all fucking died because I told them yes!"

He shushes me, holding me tighter. "Shhh, little one. I won't say it. I swear."

"Your history has conditioned you to believe that anyone you agree to a relationship with soon after passes away. And this is why you've kept that fine line between you and Brian," Doc summarizes.

I nod, wrapping my arm around Brian's neck and burying my hand in his thick hair at the back of his head. "I can't lose you, big guy. I've never…" I take a deep breath, pulling my face out of his throat to look into his beautiful blue-green eyes. "I've never l-loved anyone as much as I love you," I stutter, the word feeling foreign on my tongue. "Your job is dangerous enough without me adding my fucking curse to the mix."

All the air inside Brian's lungs rushes out, and his eyes go soft. His brow furrows with emotion as the left corner of his lips tremble slightly. "You have no idea how long I've waited to hear those words from you, lover," he growls.

"I'd guess about eleven years, seeing as that's how long it's been true," I confide. "I've loved you since the moment you asked for my camera and snapped that selfie of us in the clinic. The day you began getting your memory back."

"I remember. I still have that photo framed at home." He nods, smiling.

"I saw it on your nightstand. I'm surprised no one's ever seen it and knew about me," I murmur, fully aware I'm allowing him to distract me.

He brushes my hair back from my face, wiping the tears from my cheeks. "No one has ever been in my room except you, Clarice. Not even the guys. That's my haven, my sanctuary, and the only person I've ever welcomed into it is you. Always only you."

We get lost in each other's eyes for I don't know how long, and Doc lets us have it, not interrupting this monumental moment for the two of us. I could live in this weightless bubble for the rest of my life, ignoring the rest of the world as we hide away in this safe office where no one and nothing could hurt Brian after my confessions.

That thought brings me back to reality, and my smile fades. "But that doesn't change anything, Bri. No matter how much we may love each other, we can never officially be together."

He tucks me back into him, kissing the top of my head. "Don't worry about that right now. Nothing has to change, lover. Nothing, now that I know the truth."

I relax then, a tremendous weight lifting off my shoulders I hadn't realized was there, since I had built up my walls so long ago that they helped hold everything up.

"I can understand your fear of telling Brian about your past, Clarice, but we still have a lot more to talk about in order for you to be able to enter Club Alias. Your hour is almost up, so would you agree to come back tomorrow for your third? I can assure you the worst of it is over, now that you've gotten that off your chest," Doc prompts, and I turn to face him.

"Yeah, I think that'd be okay. Thank you, guys, for not laughing at me," I say, wiggling out of Brian's lap to sit beside him. I fan at my face, some of my sassiness coming back to life inside me as I tell Brian, "I gave you tears today. I earned the right to top tonight."

He smirks. "We'll see," he replies, surprising me. Since when does he haggle for position?

Probably since you confessed your undying love for him and he's not worried about you leaving him anymore.

"Oh, is that how it's going to be, now that I've told you how much I love you? You think you're gonna turn around and take advantage of the fact that you know I can't live without you? Well, you've got another think coming—"

He leans over and crashes his lips to mine, cutting me off and making me into a puddle of moldable goo before pulling away. "I have plans for you tonight. If you recall, I've submitted twice since you've been here. We agreed to take turns." He lifts a brow.

"But—"

"Trust me, lover. I'll make it worth your tears," he promises, and how can I argue with that?

Chapter 11

Brian

She was exactly right, my Clarice. The first thing I wanted to say after she dropped the bomb of her past on us was to assure her that nothing would happen to me. But how could I voice the one thing she said would devastate her? I could never do that. I just can't believe my sweet, strong, vibrant woman had lost so many people in her life and had managed to bury that pain and fear so deeply she was still able to function.

"Come here," I tell her, as she drops her purse onto the nightstand next to my bed.

She eyes me for a moment before deciding to obey. She shuffles over to me, where I stand at the foot of the giant bed, her head bowed, looking at her feet as she stops before me. I lift her chin with my knuckle, yet she still won't meet my eyes. I'll give her this moment to be shy, but there will be no room for it in a few minutes.

I swiftly undress, and then I grip the bottom of her shirt and tug it off, making quick work to do the same with her jean shorts and underwear. She steps out of them toward me, laying her cheek on my chest. And it's in this moment I know what I have planned for her is exactly what she needs. What we *both* need.

My heart thunders inside my chest, and I wonder if that's what she's listening to. We've never actually done what I have in mind, but I'm sure we'll figure it out just fine.

Without warning, I pick her up, and she squeaks in surprise, wrapping her legs around my waist. She holds on to me as I crawl up the mattress, and when her head hovers above the pillow, I lay us down, my weight pressing her into the white down comforter that billows up around us like a cloud. Taking her hands in mine, I trap them above her head just in case she gets any ideas about trying to flip us over so she can be on top. That's not how I want this night to go.

Leaning down, I run my short beard down then up the side of her neck, watching her skin turn to goose bumps before I nip at her earlobe. She shivers, her legs flexing around my hips. Trailing gentle pecks across her jaw, I take her lips in a kiss, pouring all the love I feel for her into it. She moans lightly, opening to me, and I dip my tongue in to taste hers. Her lips move in sync with mine, her tongue coming up to meet mine in a waltz so perfectly choreographed it could only be performed by two dancers who have been together for as long as we have. She doesn't need me to lead her. We've done this over and over so many times before we can without thinking, yet it never gets old.

I suck her bottom lip between my teeth, nibbling it before

soothing away the sting with my tongue, and as she gasps in pleasure, I begin my descent down the only body that fills my every thought, my every fantasy.

I rub my cheek against the supplest breasts I've ever felt in my life, thinking about how many times I've rested my head here while she runs her hands through my hair, comforting me after she's woken me up from nightmares filled with the ghosts of my fallen brothers. No one has ever been able to bring me peace the way she always has.

I kiss down to her stomach, licking around her navel, smiling before nipping at the softness below her belly button. So much joy has come from just sharing meals with my Clarice. And what a loss all those good memories would've been if she worried about trying to flatten this beautiful curve.

I let go of her hands, and just like I knew she would, they dive into my hair. But she must sense this night is not about power and control, because her fingers don't tug or twist the strands. She scratches her nails gently over my scalp, sending a scattering of chills down my spine as I groan against her perfect flesh.

I move lower, pressing wet kisses down her legs. She loses her grip on my hair as I sit up on my knees, pulling her leg up by her ankle so I can nip her toes, seeing her eyes shimmer as she watches me with a small smile on her face. Her hand rests lazily next to her jaw, her pretty white teeth biting lightly on her thumbnail as her dark eyes follow my every move. These little feet have traveled the world with me. We've been to so many places together, both good and bad. Both business and pleasure. And there's no one in this world I would've rather been to heaven, hell, and back with than her.

Lying back down between her legs, the backs of her thighs

resting against my shoulders, I see her pussy glistening with need, and I can't help but thrust my aching cock into the mattress. I breathe her in, her scent intoxicating; her want for me couldn't be more evident.

"You're so beautiful here, sweet Clarice," I whisper, and she whimpers, unused to hearing her name during our intimate times. Since we have a D/s sexual relationship, we call each other by the names we have for each other, the names that make us feel powerful when we wield them. But not tonight.

The first swipe of my tongue from her very center up to her clit makes her shudder, and she reaches for my head once again. She threads her fingers through my hair, only cupping my skull, as if to anchor herself in this moment. I listen to her breath as I use different techniques—tight circles around her clit, sucking at her lips, diving deep inside with my tongue. But I know her body as well as my own, and I'm already aware of what sets my girl off.

As I gently scrape my teeth over that little bundle of nerves, she sucks in a sharp breath, her muscles tightening. I glance up her delicious body to watch her beautiful face as I latch onto her most sensitive place, setting a pace with my mouth I know will make her detonate.

"Oh, God!" Her brow furrows, eyes closed tightly as her mouth forms an O as she pants. Her hips jerk, but I hold her steady as she comes, feeling the muscles of her lower half work instinctually.

When she sinks back into the covers, I lap at her juices, spreading them over her so I won't hurt her when I make her mine. Coming up on my knees, I crawl over her, hovering above her with my fists on either side of her head. Her eyes open lazily, a slow smile spreading across her face as she looks up at me.

"Definitely worth the tears," she murmurs, turning her head to press a kiss to my wrist next to her.

I chuckle, saying against her lips, "Oh, I'm not done with you yet, beautiful." She makes to sit up, but I trap her with my much bigger body, lowering to my elbows. "Uh-uh. Not tonight." I shake my head, kissing her cheek. "Tonight, we're doing something we've never done before. There is no dominance and submission." I kiss beneath her jawline. "There are no demands." I press my lips just below her ear, feeling her squirm. "There is no Mistress and her good boy." I wrap one arm beneath the small of her back, pressing her softness up against my rigid planes. "There is no Knight and his lover." I dip down and rub my bearded chin over her nipples, making her gasp. "There's only you and me, baby. Brian and Clarice."

Finally, I sink into her, my eyes wanting to close in bliss but I fight to keep them open just to watch for the—

She inhales sharply, then "Oooh."

There it is.

One of my favorite parts of our couplings. The fact that I can still get that reaction out of her every time I slide inside her tight heat never fails to make me feel like the king of the world.

My grip around her waist tightens as I thrust into her depths, making each plunge count as I go slow and deep. Her hips tilt to meet mine, and feeling myself hit her cervix, followed by hearing her startled squeak, I back off just a touch. I want this time to be all about pleasure *without* pain, no matter how much gratification both of us normally receive from it.

"Harder," she begs, but I shake my head, keeping my strokes measured.

"Not happening, my love," I tell her, and her eyes widen.

Taking her mouth in a kiss so passionate it makes me groan, I allow myself to become aware of every inch of our touching skin. "God, Clarice. I fucking love the way your soft curves cradle me like they were molded to fit only me." My hand around her back squeezes her generous hip. I lean down to suck one nipple into my mouth, letting it go with a pop. "I love the way your arms and legs wrap around me, holding me to you like you never want to let me go." I show the other nipple the same attention, my cock continuing its languid pace, and she whimpers with desire.

"Never, Brian," she whispers, and I look up at her, meeting her chocolate eyes.

"Say it again," I murmur, more of a plea than a command.

"I never want to let you go, Brian," she tells me quietly, her eyes suddenly swimming in tears.

"You never have to, baby. I'm all yours. Always have been, always will be," I say against her pouty lips. I grind against her, swiveling my hips until her eyes roll back, the tears leaking from the outer corners.

"But—"

"No. I *am* yours. And you *are* mine. Nothing else has to be said. As long as you understand that, no other words need to be spoken. There's no need for me to ask you a question that would require you to answer. Then nothing will happen to me, baby."

I can see the wheels of her mind working, fighting to concentrate through the distraction of my dick plunging deeply, filling her to the brim, as she grows wetter with every thrust. Her juices coat me from the head of my cock to my balls that press against her ass with each downward motion.

Finally, without saying the word that, in her mind, will invoke the curse that's haunted her since she was a child, she agrees. "I'm yours, Brian. And you're mine."

My heart feels like it could burst. And I'm not ashamed to admit this moment chokes me up, the ball of emotion catching in that space between my throat and chest. "I love you. So damn much," I whisper in her ear, picking up my pace only slightly.

"I love you," she breathes, digging her fingers into my back, but not her nails. I fucking love how she can read my mind, communicating without words what I wanted for us this time. Her face is a mask of concentration, and I can feel her tilting her hips into different angles, trying to find the one that will take her to the edge. After a minute more of my teasing speed, her brow furrows in frustration. "Brian, I can't…."

I've tortured her long enough. I got what I'd been craving—to actually make love to the woman of my dreams. And now it's time to give her what she needs. What we both need.

Sitting up on my knees, I drape her legs over my forearms, gripping the soft but muscular flesh of her thighs. After spreading her wide, my gaze doesn't know where it wants to settle as I thrust into her, faster and harder than before, but still not enough to register as pain. Her delicious tits bounce with every movement of my hips. Her bare pussy milks my cock as it disappears within her depths only to reappear half a second later coated in her wetness. My length has darkened, the veins bulging the closer I get to the peak. But it's when my eyes land on her face, her perfect features contorted in ecstasy, that I feel that familiar warmth start to spread throughout my center.

"I'm so close," she whines. "Please. Just a little harder. I can't… please!"

I give in, letting go of my control and pounding into her, growling in pleasure as her inner muscles clamp around me.

"Yes! Oh, God. Brian. I'm coming," she mewls, and it's my undoing.

I let her legs fall to the bed as I come forward to grip the edge of the mattress above her head as I grind my release into her, coating every solitary inch of her greedy walls with my cum. Her orgasm sucks at my cock as she moans, her arms holding onto me for dear life while she shudders in bliss.

I bury my face in the place between her neck and her shoulder, my every intake of breath filled with her scent. Her fingers on my back lighten as her aftershocks subside, her legs falling to the sides as she lets out a heavy sigh of relief.

I could stay like this forever, if I weren't afraid I'd crush her tiny frame. So instead, I finally roll us over so she's on top, sprawled across me in her most favorite place to be.

Chapter 12

Clarice

"In light of the last session, and since you two seem to have come to an understanding about the status of your *friendship*," Doc says, heavily emphasizing the word, "today I'd like for both of you to pick up where Brian left off at the end of his appointment the day you arrived."

I look over at Brian curiously. "Where did you leave off?"

"The clinic, about a week before I was released," he replies with a smile. "I was going to tell him about how my memories came back about that day the IED went off, but we ran out of time."

"Ah, nice," I state. "Go ahead, big guy."

He sits up a little straighter. "After going through her pictures again, this time on the computer so I could see details, my memory of what I saw right before the IED went off came back to me. I was in an alley between mud huts, and when I heard voices and glanced inside one of the windows, there was an American man speaking with an Afghani. From what I could gather in the seconds before all hell broke loose, the American was selling the other man an incredibly large amount of weaponry."

"I assume you told your commanding officer this information after your recollection," Doc prompts.

"Of course. And the last I heard before I got out of the military was that the IED that went off was actually set up by the American man as a security system. It was one hell of a way to warn him that people were around who might see what he was in the middle of doing," Brian says. "And the perfect distraction for him to slip away undetected."

Doc's brow furrows. "How did they figure that out?"

"Well, terrorists over there will make IEDs out of anything metal they can find. Anything that could hurt someone if projected at your body, they stick it in there. The pressure plate, if they're smart, is usually a little distance away from the explosive itself, taking into consideration their target is moving. So the walking victim would step on the plate, which would set off a timer, and then, if timed correctly, the explosion goes off once the person is near it," Brian explains, sending a shiver up my spine. He's broken this down for me before, and the next part always makes me feel nauseated.

He continues, "They like to play mind games. They don't want you actually to die. They want you to live and be miserable. They started off putting them in the ground or on the side of the road, but then they began putting them inside animals, and when us sympathetic Americans go over to the check on the poor creatures, they blow us the fuck up. And then they discovered placing the IEDs higher, where the explosion would go off near the victim's waist to emasculate them, did more psychological damage than losing a limb."

Doc closes his eyes, squeezing the bridge of his nose between his thumb and forefinger, and blows out a breath. When he seems to collect himself, he asks, "So when the IED went off, how could they tell it was the American and not one placed there by an Afghani?"

"Everything else was completely perfect—we would've never been able to tell otherwise—but the motherfucker had used an American Duracell battery in the detonator. He'd tried to place it close enough and use enough fuel to destroy all evidence completely, but lo and behold, there the little tattletale was." Brian smirks.

"And nothing has come to light about the man you saw through the window?" Doc questions, rubbing his beard.

He shakes his head. "Nope. The great mystery of my life. I've even had Seth run all sorts of checks, anyone with a history of arms dealings who have facial tattoos. I know if I saw his face I'd recognize him, but he's been able to stay off the radar for over a decade." He shrugs. "In that line of work, he's most likely already dead. What little sleep I get at night is thanks to that thought."

Doc writes something down on his notepad then shifts his intelligent eyes to me. "What about you, Clarice? What do you remember about the week before he was released?"

"Well, Doc, that last week in the clinic, we grew unbreakably closer. I quickly figured out I could talk to him about anything, and there would be no judgment, and he was genuinely interested in what I had to say. I have to admit, I was pretty addicted to the way this big, heroic man hung on my every word. I mean, after all, I had just watched him save a plethora of lives, and yet there he was, looking up to *me*?"

Brian takes my hand, bringing it to his lips to kiss my knuckles before resting it on his thigh.

I continue, "It was hard to believe the soldier in that village, taking control and executing his job flawlessly, was the same sweet, innocent young man I was getting to know in the hospital. So when our conversations started delving deeper, turning to more intimate discussions, the feeling was intoxicating. Instead of it making me feel like… I don't know, a skank for being so much more experienced than he was, it made me feel… powerful. Mature. Knowledgeable. And he never once looked at me like I was dirty. I mean, I know I'm a few years older than him, so it would be expected I'd know a couple more things about sex. But since I was already into the lifestyle by then, I had so much to talk about that he'd never even fantasized about before."

Doc nods, making notes on his pad of paper. "It's the same high a teacher gets when educating their students. It's a powerful feeling, knowing something someone else doesn't and then being able to pass on that knowledge. I'm sure you've heard the saying 'knowledge is power.'"

"Makes sense to me." I shrug.

"So did the two of you become intimate during that week?" Doc asks.

Brian shakes his head. "No. Not yet."

"Believe me, I tried," I grumble, rolling my eyes.

Brian snorts. "Hey, I was already feeling a little possessive. There weren't even any real walls. I didn't want anyone hearing or walking in and seeing any part of you."

"Ah, the innocence of babes," I singsong. "I got you to change your mind on that at the club in Vegas. You know you liked doing that flogging demonstration in front of all those people."

He lifts one shoulder. "That was a cool one-time thing, but I wouldn't want t—"

"Calm your tits, big guy. I'm only teasing. I know you've gotten more protective over the years. And I prefer it that way as well. Now, where were we? Oh yeah, the first time we did the deed." I smiled over at his handsome face before turning back to Doc. "So, shortly after his release from the clinic, he got back to work, staying there in Afghanistan, and I flew back home to New York. I'm definitely no writer, but along with my photographs and a ghostwriter, I was able to put together the article about Brian. What was meant to be a spread about our soldiers over there, fighting the war, became so much more. Even though the focus narrowed until it was mostly on Bri, it hit harder than an overview. He was a hero the people could root for, instead of their thoughts being spread thinly over a whole army. And in turn, every soldier became Brian in the minds of strangers, something more people could understand."

"Like a sports story. Tell the tale of one underdog's success, and even people who don't care about sports will suddenly become a fan long enough to enjoy the story," Doc reiterates.

"Yes! Exactly," I say excitedly, happy he understands what I'm trying to convey. "So anyway, we never stopped talking. He called when he could, and we e-mailed nearly every day. In a way, it was like an old-fashioned relationship, writing letters to each other. Talking about anything and everything. Becoming super close through our minds without our bodies being added to the mix. I think that's why we've meant so much to each other for so long, because we had that time to fully know each other on the inside before we added anything physical."

Doc nods. "Most definitely. Very astute of you to figure that out."

I beam over at Brian, and he squeezes my hand.

"A couple of months later, I came home, and she was there to meet me on the tarmac," Brian picks up.

"And *that's* when I finally got my hands on him." I grin.

Eleven Years Ago
LaRue Suites Hotel

The smile on Brian's face when he saw me standing there on the tarmac, holding my Welcome Home, Big Guy sign, was absolutely priceless. The groan he let out when the first place I stopped was Smithfield's BBQ, just like he'd dreamed about all those months ago, went straight to my lady business. And the unconscious moans that slipped from his throat as he devoured three pulled pork and coleslaw sandwiches sealed the deal for me. I wouldn't be able to rest until those sounds were caused by what I was doing to that irresistible body of his.

But it's the intoxicating nervous look on his face that pulls at my heart. No man has ever looked at me the way he does, like I'm a goddess walking the earth. He devours every word out of my mouth like he did those sandwiches, and since that was the one thing he said he couldn't wait to have once he was home again, that makes me feel pretty fucking special. And the fact that this man went through a war and still has that anxious look in his eyes because of me? I could get drunk on this feeling.

We've talked every single day since the IED went off. He knows me inside like no one else. It was so easy to talk to him, writing him e-mails as if I was just making a diary entry. Every time his response hit my inbox, I turned into a giddy schoolgirl who just received a folded note from her crush. When he'd call, my face hurt because I couldn't stop smiling the entire time we spoke.

And I've never wanted someone so badly in my life.

He drops his bag into the chair next to the window, reaching down to fiddle with the thermostat below the blinds. He peeks out the curtains, toying with the chain and testing how to open and close them. I just watch him, his tension over being alone with me for the first time in several months giving me butterflies.

Finally, I take pity on him, walking over to him until I'm within inches. He drops his hand from the curtain chain, facing me fully, meeting my eyes almost shyly. I smile gently, reaching up to trail a finger over his five o'clock shadow. "I loved the beard, but damn, Bri. You sure are handsome without it," I compliment.

He turns his mouth into my palm, kissing the center before gripping it with his fingers and moving it to the back of his head. His buzzed hair tickles my hand as I pull him down toward my lips. When his are just a breath away, he whispers, "Missed you so bad, little one," and it's my undoing. I rise to my toes, slamming my mouth to his, hooking my other arm around his neck and lifting myself until my legs lock around his waist.

His arms completely encircle me, making me feel like a tiny thing, and I love it. I've never been with a guy his size. My adrenaline rushes through my veins at the thought that he could snap me in half without breaking a sweat, yet he's so careful with me. My gentle giant. My knight in camo armor.

Yet I can't wait to corrupt him.

"I want you more than my next breath, sweet Clarice," he murmurs into my neck, making me swoon.

But I quickly shake off the feelings he's invoking inside my chest. I have to lock my heart in its steel-plated box. Not for my own protection, but for his. I can't let anything happen to this amazing man, especially anything caused by me. How careless of me would it be to fall in love with him, knowing that would be his demise?

He tries to speak again, something else that would probably pick at the lock, but I cut him off. "Shower. Now," I order, and his eyes meet mine questioningly. "We're doing this my way."

I've spent hours and countless e-mails conversing with him about my sexual preferences. He knows I need the power play. Vanilla sex just doesn't do it for me. It's too close to making love, and making love is way too dangerous. It causes hazardous feelings I can't allow.

His face expresses understanding, and he steps toward the bathroom. When we're inside, I put my feet on the floor, swiping my hair out of my face as I kick my flip-flops under the sink. He reaches for the hem of my shirt, and much to his surprise, I slap his hand, my voice stern when I bark, "No."

His neck flames above his collar, rising upward until the blush reaches his cheeks. "I'm sorry, Clarice. I thought—"

"It's not your job to think right now. It's your duty to be a good boy and follow my commands," I explain, looking him in the eye and keeping a level tone.

He seems to struggle for a moment with the thoughts inside his head, and then to my relief, he nods. "Yes, ma'am," he responds, his voice deep and sending a pleasant chill up my arms.

"Mistress," I correct, giving him the title I prefer. It makes me feel powerful, in control, especially when such a strong, virile man addresses me with it.

He licks his lips, his eyes following the movement as I do the same to mine. "Yes, Mistress."

"Good. Now, undress for me. I want to see if these months apart have changed you from the last time I got to see your beautiful body," I tell him, my voice gentler this time. His eyes soften at the compliment as his hands immediately lift to start unbuttoning his camouflaged top. I take a step back, my ass hitting the sink, and I hoist myself up to sit on the countertop while I enjoy the show. He pulls the top off, raising a brow at me in question.

I smile, impressed he's catching on so quickly. I reach out and close the door slightly, checking to make sure… and yes, just as I thought. I swing the bathroom door closed and point to the hook on the back of it.

He hangs the top there and gets back to work, taking hold of his tan T-shirt and pulling it out of his trousers. Taking hold of the back of the neck, his biceps bulge as he lifts the tee over his head, revealing miles of smooth skin. There isn't an ounce of anything but muscle beneath that perfect flesh, and my mouth waters like the first time I ever saw him naked, while he was unconscious and helpless under my care as I wiped the sweat and dirt from his body.

He bends forward a second, his hands going for his boots, but his height sucks up all the space of what seemed like a nice-sized bathroom before. Obviously not wanting to knock himself out on either the wall or the counter, he takes a seat on the side of the tub and unties the long laces of his tan boots, pulling them off and tucking his socks and laces inside them. Taking note of where I kicked mine, he puts them under the sink, lining them up neatly before standing.

His head lowered, he unbuttons his camouflaged trousers, unzipping them and hooking his thumbs in the waistband of his dark-colored boxer briefs. I don't realize I've clamped my teeth onto my bottom lip until I taste the faint tang of blood, the anticipation killing me as he lowers the fabric down his endlessly long, muscular, hairy legs, his torso hiding his hips from view until he stands up straight to step out of the rest of his clothes.

Jesus H. Roosevelt Christ, I think, a habit ever since I read

Outlander *years ago. But the delicious Scottish highlander I imagined while devouring the story had nothing on the very real, larger-than-life work of art that stands before me in all his naked, chiseled glory. No, not even my fantasies could've dreamed up a man like Brian Glover.*

I swallow thickly, making sure my voice will be strong when I'm finally able to form words. It wouldn't do for me to be a swooning schoolgirl when I'm introducing this beautiful man to the art of Dominance and submission. "Very nice. Now, start the water. You know how I like it," *I remind him, thinking back to the many showers we took together while we basically had the clinic to ourselves. He used to pick on me because I like the water so hot, saying women prefer it scalding because it reminds them of where they come from... Hell. It earned him a swift swat to his cute ass the first time he said it.*

I shed my clothes, folding them up and setting them on the closed toilet lid, my heart pounding when I see the heat enter his eyes as he turns around and sees my naked body. That's when an idea forms.

"Do you remember the first time we ever shared a shower?" *I smirk, raising a brow.*

"Of course. How could I ever forget?" *he replies, reaching up to rub the back of his neck, looking a little embarrassed.*

"Aw, don't get shy on me now." *I trail my pointer finger from the center of his chest to his navel.* "Get in." *I lift my chin toward the spray.* "Let's get you clean from that long flight." *He steps into the tub, his hand coming out for me to grasp so I don't slip as I follow him behind the curtain.* "Such a gentleman," *I coo, but then let go to grab a bar of soap from the side of the tub.*

Tearing the paper off, I get my hands wet and work it into a lather before placing my soapy palms on his muscular chest. He reaches for my hips, but I tsk, shaking my head, and he promptly drops his arms to his sides, his lips pressing together as if he's keeping himself from complaining. I giggle inside my head, getting high on the control I have over him, even though I know in the back of my mind it's the submissive, always the submissive, who is actually the one in control. They're the one allowing their Dominant to tell them what to do. They're the one who chooses how far they'll let me take them. At least, that's how it's supposed to be. I was lucky enough to have a very respectable teacher who taught me the right way.

When I'm finished with his arms and the front of his torso, I motion with my finger for him to spin around, and treat his back to a massage that soon has him slouching in relaxation. He lets out a short groan every once in a while, when I hit a particularly good spot, the sound directly linked to my pussy, making me grow wet without a single intimate touch.

As my hands trail lower, gliding over his firm glutes, the muscles flex, and he takes a step forward away from my touch. I bite my lip, forcing myself not to laugh at his masculine reaction. "No need to worry, sweet boy. I know that's way too far out of your comfort zone for our first time together," I tell him, my arm wrapping around the front of his waist as I press myself to his back, feeling him relax.

"That's way too far out of my comfort zone for our eightieth time… Mistress," he adds, and I can't help but chuckle.

"We'll see." I smile, loving the fact he's even thinking we'll be together long enough to share an eightieth time.

I clear my throat, flinching away from him at my thoughts. I can't go there. I must retain my unbreakable box. When he starts to turn to face me, I bark a little more harshly than I mean to, "Eyes forward," and he does as I command.

Lathering the soap, I squat behind him, scrubbing down his impossibly long legs from the bottom of his cheeks to his ankles, where the hair stops right before his feet. With my knees on either side of his calves, I order him to turn around, and when I glance up his towering body to meet his eyes, my inner muscles clench at the undeniable need I see there as he takes in my position.

I purposely, ever so slowly let my eyes skim down his chiseled frame, lingering on his massive erection, biting my lip when I see precum leaking from the tip. But I force myself not to give in to my desire to finally taste him, instead sitting down in the tub and making a "come here" gesture with my hands toward his right foot. He does what I want, lifting one arm to rest against the wall for balance as I massage his large foot, making sure to even get between his toes, noticing the way they flex as if it tickles. I lower that foot back to the floor, watching him shuffle it a few times to let the water rinse away the soap so he doesn't slip before giving me the other.

When I stand before him once again, I set the bar of soap in the recess of the shower wall and open the miniature shampoo bottle, signaling for him to bend down enough that I can reach the top of his short hair. I scratch my nails over his scalp, hearing him moan and seeing goose bumps spread down his bulging shoulders and biceps. His eyes are shut tightly, so I don't hide the smile that spreads across my face, enjoying that I can indulge him in such innocent pleasure.

"Rinse your hair. You can use the soap to wash anything else I might've missed." I smirk, taking in the beauty of his rippling muscles as he ducks under the spray and scrubs the suds away. When his eyes are clear, he lathers his hands and washes his backside, narrowing his eyes at me, but there's a look of amusement in his gaze. He takes the soap again, and I step back, leaning against the back wall to watch him wash around his jutting cock. As he puts the soap down and goes to turn around to rinse, I stop him. "Wait." He lifts a brow. "Back to the wall." I lift my chin to the one with the recess and handrail.

When he's there, his shoulder blades resting against the tile, he watches me, waiting for my next instruction.

"After that first shower we took together, when I came back with your towel and clothes... I saw what you were doing. I saw you finish, and the look on your face when you came. I want to see that again," I tell him, and his eyes close. I know he doesn't make a habit out of jacking off in front of people, so I allow him the time to draw on his courage, and after a moment, his big hand wraps around his girth.

My breath catches in my chest as I watch him stroke himself, the soap making the movement smooth as the lather builds with every pump of his hand. God, I could stare at him for hours he's so delicious. He has no idea what a sexy man he is.

As his brow furrows with concentration, I step forward, reaching up to position the showerhead so that it rinses the soap off as he continues to stroke. When it's all clear, I tilt the water back down then squat before him, unable to control my hunger for his taste any longer. Placing my hand over his, I hold him steady, meeting his eyes before licking the tip. His breath leaves him on a whoosh as I engulf the crown with my lips, moving his hand away to replace it with my own. I may have little to no gag reflex, but even I won't be able to take his whole cock down my throat. It matches the rest of him—larger than life and handsome as sin.

My mouth glides halfway down his length and my hand makes up for the other fraction, and I set a pace that makes him groan as I twist my palm on the upward stroke. The muscles of his thighs tense and relax as he begins to pant.

"I... you need to sto—"

I take him to the back of my throat, my hand gripping the rest of him tightly before I finally pull away, standing and reaching up to grasp the back of his head. I pull him down to my lips, kissing him deeply as I rub myself against him like a cat in heat.

He breaks our kiss to murmur against my mouth, "I'm sorry. It's been so long, and you're just... so much."

I have to forgive him for that. He's been deployed for nearly a year, hasn't been with a woman since he joined the army almost three years ago. If he feels even a fraction of the desire I feel for him, then he's probably about to explode. I can't fault him for that when I'm experiencing the same rush being in his presence after all this time.

"Bed. Now," I breathe, unable to put the force into my voice I usually do.

He turns the water off and shocks me by lifting me up. I squeak before wrapping my legs around his hips, feeling his hardness press against me as he steps out of the tub. He pulls a towel off the rack without breaking stride, opening the bathroom door and taking me over to the bed while rubbing my skin dry.

"On your back," I instruct, and he spins and falls backward, my body bouncing atop his as we land.

Suddenly, I'm in a frenzy, wanting to touch and kiss every inch of his vast amount of flesh. I worship him, taking in every hitch of his breath, every moan deep in his chest, every shudder that quakes through his big body. And when I can't take anymore, my wetness dripping down my thighs, I straddle his hips once again, taking his rigid cock in my hand and lining us up.

Just before I impale myself, I meet his ravenous stare. There's more in those blue-green orbs than just physical desire. They convey his every thought, from the love I don't want to acknowledge, to the way he clearly worships the very ground I walk on. I am a goddess in his eyes, and with that power filling my every cell, I sink down on his steely rod until I can take no more. He's the biggest I've ever taken, and he stretches me to the point of pain, but I love it. His chin points to the ceiling as he presses his head into the pillows, groaning as I rotate my hips, trying to acclimatize to his size.

With every inch of him coated in my juices, I begin to move, my hands balancing on his rippling abs as I lift and lower myself over and over again. And as my muscles relax around him, I add a rocking motion to the up and down, making my heart stop for a full second at how fucking glorious the feeling is as he hits that magical place inside me.

"Oh, fuck," he growls, his head lifting to watch our connection before meeting my eyes. His brows are low over his swirling eyes, his mouth slightly open as he pants for breath. "I don't know… can't hold off much longer, baby."

"Mistress," I correct weakly, the roller coaster inside me ready to click in place at the top of the highest peak.

My hips pump faster as he instinctively lifts his to meet mine, and at his hissed, "Fuck me… Mistress…" that's when the brakes finally let go, and I fall over the edge.

My inner walls barely have room to ripple around him he fills me so much, and I have to catch myself from falling forward as the orgasm overwhelms my every sense. As I scream in absolute ecstasy, never before experiencing anything like the feelings consuming me now, that's when I hear his grunt of relief, every muscle in his body going lax beneath me.

I collapse on his chest, struggling to catch my breath, and feel his arms wrap around me. I close my eyes, savoring the safety and care I sense cocooned in his embrace. He breathes deeply at the top of my head, his grip tightening, and suddenly rolls us over, his weight pressing me into the mattress.

He smiles down into my face, but then his eyes startle. "Oh shit. We didn't use a—"

"No worries, big guy," I tell him calmly, switching back to my usual nickname for him since the "scene" is complete. "I'm part of a club that requires monthly testing and I'm all clear. You're in the army and haven't had sex in years. They test y'all regularly, so I'm not concerned."

"But what about… ya know… getting pregnant," he whispers the last part, making me burst out laughing.

"Who do you think is gonna hear you in here, you dork?" I ask, looking left and right as much as I can with his large body holding me down. "I'm on the pill." His relief is evident as he smiles once more, kissing the corner of my mouth sweetly. "And as long as you promise I'm the only one you'll go bareback with, we can make this our normal." That statement surprises even me as it slips past my lips. I've never not used protection before, but with Brian, the thought hadn't even entered my mind. I trust him that much.

"Lover," he says, the new endearment making my breath hitch, "you're the only one I'll be—"

I cut him off, the emotions growing too thick around us. "Shhh, don't worry about all that now." I wiggle beneath him. "My feet are falling asleep. I think your big dick is cutting off my circulation," I tell him with a playful grin, and we spend the next half hour cleaning each other up once again in the hotel shower with its never-ending supply of scalding water.

"You seem to have a very firm grasp of what it takes to be a successful Dominant, Clarice. I'm impressed," Doc compliments, and I squeeze Brian's hand, feeling warm from the recollection of our first time.

"Like I said, I had a great teacher. I don't know what I would've done without her," I state.

Doc makes a note. "We'll save that for your next session. But with the little time we have left for today, let's move forward in the timeline instead of backward. Brian told me recently that you were there when I contacted him about joining my security team. Can you tell me what you remember about that?"

"Oh, there was no question in my mind. Once you explained what your team was all about, I told him he should go for it. He was already a little worried about what line of work he'd be able to do once he got out of the military. He was questioning what he should go to school for with his GI bill. I could tell he was stressing about what direction to move in, and your offer seemed to be fate dropping into his lap," I explain.

"And about the same time is when you got the other job offer as well," Brian reminds me.

"Oh yeah!" I nod, smiling widely. "Like two days after he got your e-mail, I was hunted down by the company I work for now, and it just so happened to be only three hours away from here. It was torturous only getting to see him every few months, since I lived in New York and him in North Carolina, especially since I traveled out of the country so much for work. So we made the decision together. He'd join your team, and I'd take the job within driving distance of him. And even better, it nearly doubled my salary, and I didn't have to take 'out of the country' jobs if I didn't want to. I don't *have* to go where they need me to. There is always a list of shoots where a professional photographer is needed, and we just pick the ones we want to take."

"That sounds a lot like your parents' occupations as flight attendants. Don't they make their own schedules in a similar way?" Doc asks.

"Exactly. My apartment is just a mile away from the company's hub and within minutes of the closest airport, so I can hop on a plane the same day a job is needed and have little worry about travel arrangements. And my parents can hop on a flight and come see me whenever we want. It's been wonderful these last few years."

"You know… all of your work stuff can be done online. *And…* our airport is only half an hour away," Brian inserts, and my eyes turn to him in surprise.

"Ya don't say," I murmur, a smile tickling at my lips.

"I'm just sayin'," he adds.

"And I think I'm picking up what you're throwing down, big guy."

"I mean, you're barely at your apartment anyway. Think of all the money you'd save if you didn't have to pay all that rent." He turns an innocent look my way, and I raise a brow.

"It would be nice not to pay nine-hundred bucks a month for a space I usually use as just a storage unit," I agree. "Ya gonna help me find a place to be my mothership?"

His eyes go soft, making those fucking butterflies take off in my vagina again. "I've already got a place in mind, lover. And I have a distinct feeling you're gonna love it."

We go quiet after that, our minds filled with the possibilities his unspoken offer has conjured. Finally, it's Doc who breaks the silence. "Well, it seems you two have quite the conversation to have. Your hour is up, Clarice. I look forward to seeing you tomorrow."

"You too, Doc," I reply, Brian standing and tugging me to my feet. He seems eager to leave, and I can only imagine why.

Chapter 13

Brian

Did that really just happen? Did I seriously just throw caution to the wind and suggest Clarice move in with me? Sure, I didn't actually say the words, but she knew exactly what I was saying. And she didn't shut me down. She didn't change the subject or blow me off. In fact, it was the complete opposite response than what I'm used to from her. I'm still unaccustomed to this openness about our love for each other. So the fact that the suggestion fell from my lips so easily came as a surprise. I hadn't even realized what I'd told her until she was already obviously considering it.

I look across the booth at the beauty before me. She's leaned back in her seat, blindly reaching for french fries and munching on them while scrolling on her phone, laughing every once in a while and turning it to face me so I can read the funny memes she comes across. When she stops for a moment, turning the cell sideways, I watch her perfect features go from concentration to smiling widely, until tears fill her eyes and one spills over. I know that look. I know that reaction. Only two things get to her like that.

"Soldiers coming home, or dog adoption success story?" I ask, reaching out across the table and swiping the tear away, rubbing it between my fingers to absorb it into my skin.

She sniffles. "Dogs reacting to soldiers returning home."

I chuckle. "A double whammy then. You're such a sap."

"Your face is a sap," she replies snidely.

"Ooh, sick burn," I tease. "Hey, devices down." My arm jets out to tap on her screen, making her squeal.

"Bri! You're gonna make me like a frenemy's post!" she whines, and I shake my head.

"Why do you follow anyone who you wouldn't want to like their updates?" I ask, lifting a brow.

She shakes her head at me, finally meeting my eyes. "It's called a hate-follow. Duh. You follow them to see what they're up to so you can totally hate on them in your mind."

"And why would you want to do that?" I swear women confuse the fuck out of me sometimes.

"Because it makes you feel better about your own life, or it pushes you to do better," she tries to explain, but I still don't get it.

"Alrighty then," I murmur, but thankfully she locks her screen and tosses the phone in her bag, giving me her attention.

She flips her hair over her shoulder. "Plus, before I got distracted by the ad of the exact Hufflepuff shirt I was thinking about buying not three hours ago, I was checking my e-mails to see when my lease is up on my apartment."

My heart thuds in my chest, not expecting this sudden turn in conversation. "And?" I prompt.

She giggles. "Apparently it's been up for seven months, and I've just been on a month-to-month basis. I didn't respond to one of the e-mails back then, and so they automatically moved me to month-to-month, and if I want out of the rental, I have to give them one month's notice. And since I paid first and last month's rent when I first moved in, it's all taken care of when I'm ready to move."

"Seriously?" My eyes bug out.

She grins. "Seriously."

My mouth opens and closes a few times, unsure how to move this talk along to the part where I ask her if she'd like to move—

"So when am I moving in, big guy?"

"This is potentially your last session, Clarice. How are you feeling today?" Doc asks the next morning, and I glance over to see her beam that beautiful smile of hers to where he sits across from us in his leather chair.

The past two days have been nothing but magical, getting to convey my love to Clarice without her shying away. Hearing those three words from her lips aimed at me has been a dream come true. And ever since we discussed her moving in, I've been floating on a cloud, no matter how much of a pussy that makes me sound. But I know the men who I surround myself with understand exactly how I feel, since they're the same way with their women.

"I'm awesome, Doc," she replies. "Looks like you'll be seeing a lot more of me come next month. And instead of that visitor's pass for the club, I'm going to need a full membership."

"So I guess congratulations are in order." Doc leans forward, his hand held out for me to clasp and shake before he squeezes my arm in brotherly affection.

Clarice clears her throat. "Ummm… I'm pretty sure the congratulations should go to me. I'm the one getting a brand-new bomb-ass house and dick on command. No more weeks in between orgasms for me."

I snort, and Doc lets out a loud, quick laugh, bringing a grin to Clarice's face.

"So, today you wanted me to tell you about how I got introduced to BDSM, correct?" she prompts. That's my girl, taking control of the situation as always.

Doc sobers. "Yes. Backtracking to what you told me in session two, you lost your virginity to the man who became your fiancé before his passing," he says softly. At her nod, he continues. "And according to your recollection, that was the last actual relationship you ever had."

"Correct," she states. "Obviously, I went into a deep depression after losing him. I was only twenty-one at the time. Probably way too young to be getting married anyway, but that didn't make it hurt any less. They let me mourn for a long time, but then my girlfriends started taking me out a lot, to get me out of the house we all shared near campus. I began partying and drinking, going out to clubs and dancing. A year and a half after he died, I finally slept with someone else." She side-eyes me, but I make sure not to react. I don't want to discourage her from being open and honest.

"It didn't go very well. For me at least," she adds. "It felt all right, but I didn't orgasm. And thinking it was a fluke, because I never had any problems getting off with Zachary, we did it again. But still, no O." She lifts her hands in an I-don't-know gesture.

"Maybe it was the guy. So… I did it with someone else. And then someone else. And then a couple more someone elses." Her hands drop back into her lap. "Still. No. Orgasm. So that meant it was me, right?"

She widens her eyes at Doc then at me before sighing, facing forward again. "So one of my roommates suggested I go to her therapist. And this therapist, she was freaking awesome. Basically the female version of you, Doc. After several sessions, attempting to work through the other issues I was trying to bury—and you guys know how that went—I asked if could focus on the sexual issue, since it was the most frustrating out of everything. In my head, if I could solve this small problem, it would give me the confidence to tackle the bigger ones."

Doc makes a note. "That's a rational line of thinking. Please, continue."

She sits back on the couch, pulling her feet up beneath her and letting her knees fall sideways over my thigh. "Apparently she'd already been thinking about this, because she had an immediate solution. She asked 'Clarice, have you ever heard of BDSM or Dominance and submission?' And I was like, 'You mean like *The Secretary?*'" She chuckles, smiling over at me. "She told me that she could see me benefiting from the role of a Dominant during sexy times. Of course, I laughed in her face. I was in no way turned on by the thought of spanking or whipping people. Hurting someone was the last thing that would ever bring me pleasure. After all, I was a fucking Black Widow. Anyone who loved me ended up dead."

She snorts, rolling her eyes. "And plus, weren't submissive men these weak little boys with mommy issues? I've always been attracted to alphas, men who embodied everything that was male, without being a misogynistic dickwad, of course." She lifts her arm behind my head and starts playing with my hair there. "But she assured me, that wasn't always the case. And I soon learned she was absolutely correct."

"So your therapist was the one who introduced you to BDSM?" Doc prompts.

"Yes, because come to find out, she was also a sex therapist who worked for a club about an hour away from where we lived. And soon, I was taking training courses from her there. And after being partnered with a guy who was definitely not a weak little boy, and experiencing the power I felt when he submitted to me, the big O returned!" she says dramatically, lifting her hands to the ceiling.

"So you were strictly trained as a Domme?" Doc asks.

She nods. "Yes."

"Yet sometimes you submit to Brian. How did that happen?"

"Well, I knew from day one that he only submitted to me for my pleasure. He didn't care either way. He just wanted to be intimate with me. The D/s thing was something I needed to get pleasure. I mean… until a couple nights ago." She smiles shyly over at me, and I run my finger down the bridge of her nose before kissing her forehead.

"What happened a couple nights ago?" Doc interrupts.

She faces him, a blush on her cheeks. "We made love. Just plain vanilla-y goodness. And I had one of the best orgasms of my life," she admits.

Doc nods, making a note. "Emotions were high after that session. You were probably feeling the same rush during your lovemaking that you usually feel during a scene using power and control."

"Makes sense," she replies. "Anyway, that was our norm for the next few years, while he was still in the army. He was the perfect sub. Anytime I wanted to play and experiment, he never shied away. He always let me try things at least once, deciding then if he liked it or not and wanted a repeat. But then after he took the job with you, and I started meeting him on his missions, I thought about how unfair it was that he always gave in to anything I wanted to make me happy. Was there anything he wanted to try that would fulfill a fantasy of his?"

"That would've been around the same time Seth had the idea to build Club Alias, correct?" Doc questions.

"Exactly, and since your team would be acting as Dominants at the club, it only sealed the deal in my mind. I needed to submit to Brian, my Knight—" Her hand that had gone lax behind me begins toying with my hair again. "—so he could be complete too. I made the offer, turning it into a game, that when he completed his mission, he would earn my submission. So really, I was still in control. And after the first time, I found I really, *really* enjoyed it as well."

"You're able to reach orgasm when you are the submissive?" Doc clarifies.

"Oh yes. I don't think I would if it were anyone else. But Brian becoming Knight really does something for me."

I bury my face in the side of her neck then, breathing her in, and she giggles at the scratch of my beard against her soft skin.

"Down, boy. We gotta be good so I can earn my cool kids' card," she says, leaning away with a grin.

"Well, with all the information you've given me here, I'm very comfortable giving the seal of approval for your membership, Clarice. It seems to me your reasons for being part of a BDSM lifestyle is completely healthy and there aren't any deeper issues we need to work on before allowing you to enter the club," Doc says, putting his pad of paper and pen on his side table.

Her jaw goes slack. "For real?"

"I mean... unless there's anything else you need to divulge—"

"No! No. That's it. I swear," she tells him excitedly, her smile beaming over at me.

"Brian will, of course, act as your sponsor. It'll be nice to see him actually participating and getting to enjoy the business he helped build," he says, and I snort.

And I make Clarice laugh and Doc choke on his spit before we leave when I ask him, "Who's gay now?"

Chapter 14

Clarice

"Hey, Bri?" I gallop down the stairs from where I took a call on my cell a few minutes ago in the bedroom. It was about work, so Brian gave me some privacy and went down to the living room to start up Netflix so we could continue binge-watching *The Sinner*. We're completely obsessed. "Would you be terribly upset if I took off for just a couple hours?"

"What's going on?" he asks.

"My friend asked if I could go photograph a real estate property that's about an hour from here. I'm way closer than she is, so she said she'd pay a pretty hefty amount if I saved her the trouble," I explain, and he shrugs.

"Just there, snap some pics, and come back?" he clarifies.

I nod. "Yep, that's it. I'll be back in time for our first night at the club." My face splits into a grin so wide my cheeks cramp. I'm so freaking excited about tonight, finally getting to see my guy's club.

"I don't mind at all. I have a little bit of paperwork to do anyway. I was just putting it off so we could get to the next episode," he replies, and lean over him to kiss him sweetly on the lips.

"Perfect. I'm just going to grab my camera and then I'll be back by…" I look at my cell to see what time it is now—a little after 4:00 p.m. "Sevenish."

"Okay, lover. You gonna eat on the road, or you want me to wait for you?" He trails his finger along my jaw when he stands, tilting my head back and bending down to give me a proper goodbye kiss that leaves me a little breathless.

I lick my lips to steal his taste. "Wait for me. I'm still full from our late lunch."

"Yes, ma'am," he murmurs, making my heart thump before I finally pull myself away to go collect my camera bag from upstairs.

An hour and fourteen minutes later, I pull onto the property my friend gave me the address for and look around. "Creeeeepy," I sing aloud, taking in all the warehouses spread as far as the eye can see. Thankfully, a number is painted clearly on each building, and I slowly drive over the gravelly lot in order to find number 7423. The place seems deserted. There are a few cars at other buildings, but I suppose, since it's after five, everyone has gone home if any of these warehouses are places of business.

I hop out of the car, my camera bag hooked over my shoulder, and make my way to the regular door at the end of a row of garage style ones. Typing in the code she'd texted me for the key box, it clicks open, and I slide the key out, unlock the door, and immediately flip on the lights. I would absolutely shit myself if I had to be in this spooky ass building in the dark by myself.

"Talk about *Saw* vibes," I mumble to myself, looking around at all the chain-link cages along the walls. I glance up and see a catwalk, several office areas on both the bottom and top floors, while the tall two-story center area remains completely open. "Imma just get this over with."

I pull my camera out of the bag, flip it on, and start snapping. I walk quickly, making sure to get different angles of all the cages, carefully climbing the metal stairs and taking photos all the way to the top until I reach the catwalk. I hold the railing to get to the center and try to keep my vertigo under control as I aim my lens up toward the ceiling and then down to get shots of the floor and the cages from above. The offices are next, and then finally I make it to a smaller set of stairs and a door that leads out onto the roof of the building. It's locked, but luckily the same key for the main door opens this one as well.

I step into the evening air, gazing out at all the warehouses around me. Up here, it's not so unnerving. It's actually quiet and peaceful, no city noises, since we're completely surrounded by woods. I walk slower up on the flat roof, enjoying the silence interrupted only by the sound of my shutter going off when I take a picture. I spend several minutes overlooking the buildings around me, knowing I'm going to have to be cooped up in my car for another hour to get back to Brian.

A smile pulls at my lips thinking about him. Tonight will be a big night for us. I've always wanted to see his club but never had the balls to invite myself. And I'm sure Brian never asked me to come before because he knew what it would take for me to gain entrance. I'm almost certain that if I'd gone to Doc *before* the last three missions I went on with Brian, I wouldn't have returned for the second session, much less completed all four while telling them about the boys and men of my past. And now that it's over with, everything out in the open, finally being able to admit the way I feel to Brian, I can't wait to submit to him in his club. Not only because it'll be my first time there, but because it'll be *his* first time actually being able to use his own facility.

After a few more minutes up on the roof, I head toward the doorway, ready to make my way home. I'm just about to dissect the fact that I'm already thinking of Brian's house as *home*, when a loud bang catches my attention. I turn in the direction it came from, curiosity getting the best of me. Another bang sounds from the warehouse next to the one I'm on top of, and I tiptoe to that side. Edging closer as quietly as I can, I peek over the side and see the sound must've been two of the garage doors opening.

Standing in front of two black SUVs are three men. I can't make out what they're saying, but one of the men seems to be telling the other two to load up whatever is inside the warehouse. Just then, a delivery truck pulls in, the wrap displaying fruits and vegetables with the company's name, so I assume they've got to load the back full of produce to drop off at some stores and restaurants.

Oh, how very wrong my assumption is.

The man giving the orders stands by the back of the delivery truck, and as the others bring out the crates, he has them open each one to count what's inside. And what's inside is definitely not apples and bananas. No. The crates are full of rifles, handguns, and what I'm guessing are hand grenades if my vast recollection of war movies and time overseas is anything to go by.

"What the fuck?" I whisper to myself. Could this be the supply warehouse for a gun store? Or maybe they're actually toys and they're getting ready for a reenactment? No. No way. Not if they're loading everything up into a fucking turnip truck. There has to be something very illegal going on, and with that amount and type of weaponry, something really bad could be going down. I'd be stupid not to say anything.

But being who I am, I can't just run and tattle. I need photographic evidence. And without thinking, I lift my viewfinder to my eye and snap photos in rapid succession just as one of the men opens one of the crates for the leader to see inside.

The loud click of the shutter going off sounds like a scream in the otherwise dead silence, and that, along with my hissed "Shit!" draws the attention of the men below. As fast as I can, I jerk away from the edge, praying with all my might that they didn't see me. But as I hear the crunch of the gravel moving closer to my warehouse, I know they're coming to check out what they heard.

"Fuck my life," I murmur, and hurry to the opposite side of the roof. I glance down, seeing my car two stories below. I'd hurt myself for sure if I tried to jump down, but there's absolutely nowhere to hide up here or even inside the warehouse, since it's completely empty. I look around, my heart pounding in my ears as I try to figure out what to do, and that's when I spot it. A metal set of stairs, a fire escape.

Not wanting to alert the men of my escape route, I hook my camera around my neck so I can grasp onto both sides of the handrail, lifting most of my weight in order to keep my footfalls quiet as I make my way down the steps. And just because that's who I am as a person and I don't want my friend to get into trouble, as fast as I can, I put the key back into the lockbox, hustling to my car, and push the button to start it. I throw it into reverse and stomp on the gas just as two men round the building. When they see me speeding away, my own eyes widen in fear as they draw handguns out from around their backs.

"Oh, fuck!" I scream, flooring the gas pedal.

As the first shots ring out, I swing my car around the end of the warehouse, stomp on the brake long enough to switch into drive, and take off as fast as my wheels will take me.

My adrenaline is rushing so badly I don't think to call for help, not the police, not Brian, no one. All I can think about is, what if they've jumped into their SUVs and are now in pursuit?

Chapter 15

Brian

My front door slams open almost a full hour before I expect Clarice to be back, and automatically, my hand draws the pistol from the top drawer of my desk, aiming directly at the doorway as my woman flies through it.

She skids to a stop, raising her hands in surrender. "Whoa, big guy. I've already been shot at once today. Can we not have a repeat please?"

I immediately lower the weapon back into the drawer, striding over to where she's shaking like a leaf. "What are you talking about? What happened?"

She spends the next few minutes animatedly giving me a play-by-play of what went on at the warehouse, her voice rising in hysteria as she nears the end of her story. "And then the fuckers shot at me! I hightailed it the hell out of there, racing down the highway like a bat out of hell, so I pray to all that's holy they weren't able to follow me."

I grab her hand, spinning her around and pulling her through the doorway. "Let's go. We gotta take those photos to Seth and figure out what the fuck is going on." Turning on the security system, I lock the door behind us, opening the passenger door of Clarice's car for her since she's parked behind my truck. I hop in the driver seat, and in fifteen minutes, we're at the club. "Not exactly how I dreamed about you seeing Alias for the first time, but it's not open yet, so at least you won't get the full effect and ruin it."

"If I don't get killed by arms dealers before I ever get to enjoy it," she murmurs, taking hold of my hand as I unlock the blacked-out glass door and pull it open.

"I'm not going to let anything happen to you, lover," I promise, hurrying her through the entryway that usually has someone checking IDs and membership cards, but it's too early for that. We run up the stairs, through the quiet, empty main room of the club, past the booths and bars, and over to the far right wall to a set of stairs that lead up to the hall of offices.

The place is a ghost town, but I know Seth's hermit ass is most likely at home, which happens to be the loft at the end of the hallway—for now. I'm sure now that Twyla is pregnant, she might be able to pull him out of his nerd cave and into a bigger place.

I push the button, standing in front of the camera. Sure enough, Seth's face appears on the screen. "Well, hey there, you sexy beast. To what do I owe this surprise visit?" he asks, his smile wide.

"Need you and your spaceship, man. Let us in," I tell him, my voice serious.

He unlocks the door right away and welcomes us inside with a gesture of his hand. "What's the matter? Hey, Clarice."

"Hey." She gives him a wavering smile, still clearly shaken up. She goes to sit at the kitchen counter, where Twyla is perched on a barstool, looking concerned.

"You all right?" I hear her ask my girl, but I don't hear her response as I stride over to the far wall of the loft, where Seth's huge computer setup is arranged.

He takes a seat in the futuristic looking chair, swinging it around to face the multiple monitors, wiggling his mouse to wake everything up. "Okay, hit me," he says, looking up to meet my eyes.

I pull Clarice's camera out of its bag, removing the memory card out of its slot and handing it over. "The last few pictures will be an arms deal going down at a warehouse next door to where my woman was taking photos for her real estate friend. They saw her, probably also have her license plate number now. I need to find out what I'm dealing with before they have a chance to even think about fucking with her."

He nods, loading the card and pulling up the pictures, displaying them across the screens.

I stumble back a step.

My mouth gapes open before my jaw slams shut.

Disbelief and fury fills every crevice of my mind and stomach.

I blink just to be sure my eyes aren't deceiving me, but sure enough, the image is perfect and clear, especially as Seth zooms in closer.

There, standing beside a produce truck, bending over a crate and inspecting its contents, is a man with a tattoo of a bow and arrow on his temple.

The man whose face still haunts my dreams over a decade after I first saw him in that godforsaken mud hut.

The very man who had killed and maimed my team in Afghanistan.

"Mother*fucker.*"

Thirty minutes later, everyone is piled into Seth and Twyla's loft, Clarice's photos printed out and lining the kitchen island.

"The angle she took these pics from, we can't see the license plate of the produce truck, but we can make out most of the letters on the two SUVs. I'm running a check on those to see what I can find. Shouldn't take long," Seth tells the group.

"What's important is finding that truck before it makes its delivery. God only knows what they've got planned for all that weaponry. It could be another overseas deal, or heaven forbid, it could be to supply an attack planned right here in the States," Doc says.

"Are there any security cameras on the property?" Corbin asks in Seth's direction.

"Surprise, surprise. All systems are a go except around building 7422. I was immediately able to tap into the security feed. Even rewound it back and saw our little FBI agent on top of the roof—which is funny, since her name's… yeah. Not the time," Seth replies, stopping his line of thought at my glare.

"The truck didn't pass by any active cameras on the way in?" Astrid asks, stepping between Twyla and Doc and checking out the photos.

"The truck itself must have an EMP or an electromagnetic pulse device. The cameras flickered off as soon as it got near them and then turned back on when it was out of range. So unless you were actually watching the feed, you'd never even notice the system was interrupted, and the truck is like a ghost," Seth explains, causing a collective grumble to spread across our group.

I run my hand through my hair in frustration. "Well, it looks like the only option is to just go back to the warehouse and see if they've left any breadcrumbs." I turn to the guys. "Guard her as if she were yours," I tell them, my face a mask of dead-seriousness.

"Whoa, hold on a second, big guy," Clarice inserts. "You're not doing this alone. I'm going with you."

I shake my head. "Like hell you are. What have I told you over and over during my missions? You stay where you're safe so I can concentrate and get the job done. If not, all I'll be able to worry about is you."

"Fuck that, Brian! No way. You can't go by yourself. Especially after I just told you—" Her throat clogs, and she visibly swallows, tears filling her chocolate eyes.

My fierce expression softens instantly, and I walk around the island to wrap her in my arms. "How many times do I have to tell you, lover? I'm invincible," I murmur against the top of her head.

"You're not though. No one is. Especially any man I love. Please, Bri. Don't go alone," she pleads, her tears soaking through my shirt, breaking my heart.

"He won't be going alone," Corbin says, and I look up to meet his stony face. "Those were my brothers this fucker blew up too. If I hadn't been on another assignment, I would've been in that alley that day." Vi gasps from the stool she's sitting on, holding baby Vincent. Corbin wraps his arm around his wife's shoulders. "The two of us will follow the trail and get everything taken care of. Together. We will have each other's back. Everyone else, stay *in this loft* in case they're able to track Clarice's car."

When he says that, I feel like a complete idiot for driving us here in her vehicle. But I wasn't thinking straight after she'd just told me she'd been shot at.

"Not a problem. No one is getting into this bad boy," Seth says, gesturing toward the steel-plated door. "We'll lock the club down as well and send out a text to members letting them know we're closed for the night."

"And Clarice's car is in the underground garage. No one will see it," Doc reminds me, making me feel a little better about my blunder.

Seth's computer makes a noise, drawing everyone's attention as he jogs across the loft. "We have a hit. The first SUV's plates were matched, and the vehicle is currently two miles from the warehouse on a private airfield."

"But they weren't loading the weapons into the SUV. They were putting them in the delivery truck," Clarice states, looking up at me.

"We won't know anything until we get there. But we need to go now if we stand any chance of stopping them," I reply. "Seth, keep us updated."

"Always, bro," he calls.

I see Corbin leaning in to whisper something to Vi, kissing her goodbye, and I look down into Clarice's shimmering eyes. "I promise nothing is going to happen to me, baby. There's no way in hell I'll let anyone take me away from you, not after we finally just got each other the way I've always dreamed."

Her breath comes out stuttered before she blinks back her tears and nods, wiping her cheeks. She sniffs, clearing her throat and putting on a brave face. She gives me her beautiful smile, reaching up to cup my cheek in her tiny hand. "I believe you, big guy." Her voice tells me she's trying to make herself believe the statement as much as me. "Now kiss me. And when you get back, I'll give you a reward."

There's my girl. I pull her up to press my lips to hers, putting every ounce of devotion inside me into that kiss. When I finally pull away, I tell her I love her, and Corbin and I leave the loft, making our way to our offices and stock up on what we need to bring.

Chapter 16

Brian

"There's no record of this guy anywhere. Facial recognition didn't pull up a fucking thing," Corbin says from the passenger seat as we near the warehouse.

"So the operation must have their own Seth. You can't find a single thing about any of us on the Internet anywhere. I mean, if he can wipe us from every military record, getting rid of every damn sign of our existence except for hard copies of that article Clarice wrote about me more than a decade ago, then it's not surprising this fucker has his own computer genius," I reply.

"True, and if this guy's been able to stay afloat for this long, then he's not dumb. He'd definitely have someone like that on the payroll." Corbin leans forward to look out the windshield as we slowly approach a warehouse two over from the one in question. If anyone is there, we don't want to alert them to our presence. We get out of Corbin's truck, which I drove so he could communicate with Seth on the way here, knowing if I tried to sit idly by it would make me insane.

We round the corner of one building and then another, using hand signals engrained in our brains from our military training. There are no vehicles outside the warehouse, but that doesn't mean someone isn't inside. Circling the building, Corbin gestures to the fire escape, and we make our way quietly up the metal steps to the second level. Instead of going to the roof, which would probably make way more noise going through the metal door there, we stop at the wide window that leads into an office space.

Corbin lifts up on the bottom of the window and finds it locked. But this isn't our first rodeo. He pulls a glasscutter out of one of the cargo pockets of his pants along with a tiny spray bottle of kerosene. Dousing the tip of the tool with the liquid, he cuts a space just large enough for one finger to reach through and flip the lock open. Within minutes, we're inside the office, and we can see the warehouse is completely dark.

Instead of flipping on the lights, we use small LED flashlights that fill the space with a bright glow so we can see where we're going, and as we exit the office and point the lights down toward the first floor from the walkway leading to the stairs, what we find makes us breathe a "Holy fuck" in unison.

Rows upon rows of weapons, from pistols to machine guns. Hand grenades, rifles of all makes and models. It looks like every gun show in the United States has chosen this particular warehouse to store their inventory. If I weren't on a mission to kill the fucker who murdered my friends and shot at my woman, I would have a massive boner in the presence of all this artillery.

"Well, no one is here. Should we move on to the airport?" I ask Corbin.

He nods, practically drooling over the sniper rifle he just spotted. He trails his finger over the stock and down the barrel.

"Don't even think about it, man," I tell him.

His eyes shimmer as he takes it into his hands, lifting the site to his eye. "But—"

"But nothing. You have plenty. The one you have in the truck makes that one look like a paintball gun," I remind him.

"One cannot have 'plenty' when speaking of weaponry. Have I taught you nothing?" he asks, even as he sets the rifle back in its place.

Instead of crawling back out the window, we save time by exiting through the door nearby after making sure no one had shown up in the few minutes we'd been inside. When we're back in the truck, Corbin pulls up the directions on the GPS. As we're exiting the warehouse district through the gates, a call rings through the Bluetooth.

"Seth, whatcha got?" I ask after pushing the Answer button on the steering wheel.

"I have visuals on this fucker at the airport. He's there and about to take off. Get your asses there immediately," he states, and I punch the gas.

"We're one mile out," I growl, and Corbin unbuckles his seat belt, climbing over the center console to the back seat. "Little problem, Seth. Even if we take him out, he's obviously got a hacker on his team. We're gonna need to find—"

"Already on it, bro. He may be good, but he ain't me. I've almost got the encryption decoded that's scrambling his IP address, which would lead directly to his location. Also, you and Corb have been completely erased from the warehouse district's security feed. You were never there." Excitement fills his voice and I shake my head with a cautious smile.

"I knew we kept you around for a reason," I tell him, adrenaline pumping through my veins as signs for the airport come into view.

"There's a back road that runs parallel with the section for private planes. With Corbin there, you won't have to get handsy like you tend to prefer. I'd go one shot, one kill on this bad boy," he tells me. "With him already on the jet, we don't want to take any chances of him getting away."

As much as I'd love to have words with the fucker who killed my fellow soldiers and injured even more, not to mention the ones who've been shot by guns he's provided opposing forces, I cannot let him escape. I'll be at peace knowing he died by Corbin's flawless marksmanship.

"Agreed," I reply to Seth, and Corbin's hand comes over my shoulder from the back seat, a bullet squeezed vertically between the pads of his thumb and forefinger.

"Looky what I swiped," he says, and I glance in the rearview mirror to see his giddy expression.

"What is it?" Seth asks through the Bluetooth.

"Jacked a bullet from the warehouse. When forensics compares it to the ones at the warehouse, they'll see it matches and think one of his guys turned on him," Corbin answers as I pull to the side of the road along the fence at the backside of the airport. The sun has set, and with our headlights out, we're basically invisible in the wooded coverage.

"Pretty *and* smart," Seth coos, and I see Corbin roll his eyes in the reflection before opening the door, walking around the front of the car, and disappearing from view in the darkness. We disconnect our call as I hold my breath, waiting for Corbin to make his move.

After a moment, my ribs can barely contain my heart as it tries to escape my chest at the sound of the plane starting its engines.

"I've got him in my sights," Corbin murmurs through my earpiece, making me almost jump out of my skin.

This anxiety is a new thing for me. I've only felt it once before when that fuckstick tried to shove Clarice into his trunk in Raleigh. It was personal, unlike most of my missions. So it explains why I'm having this reaction. This is very *personal*. That IED could've easily exploded and killed me had I not gone in another direction to secure the building. Those were *my* teammates he maimed and killed. It's probably a blessing Corbin came with me to get the job done, because if I were in that fucker's presence right now, there's no way I'd have the self-control to make this look like an accident or like one of his goons turned on him. There would be no hiding the fact that I was the one who murdered the son of a bitch, because I would bathe in his blood.

In the next second, I hear a soft clang of metal as Corbin's silencer muffles the sound of his shot, followed by a woman's scream—probably a flight attendant aboard the private jet. Corbin's head pops up over the hood as he stands from his position on the ground, carrying his sniper rifle in one hand while brushing the dirt and leaves off his front, his expression calm, as if he didn't just take the life of the man we've been searching for since our early twenties. At thirty-two years old, I'll finally be able to sleep like a baby.

When he climbs back into the truck, he tosses me something small and hot as it lands in my open palm. The metal casing of the bullet. A weight lifts off my shoulders and my heart finally calms. A sense of peace washes over me as I nod at him.

Thirty minutes into our drive home, Seth calls again. "Found him," he says by way of greeting.

"The hacker?" I clarify, rolling up my window so I can hear him better.

"Yup. FBI are on their way to his location. Had a little fun with him, because that's just who I am as a person."

I can't help but chuckle. "What did you do?" I scold.

"When I tapped into his computer, he was in the middle of tracking your girl's car." His words immediately wipe the smile from my face as my gut grows cold. "I made it show that her vehicle was in Thailand. No worries, bro. Anyway, I fucked with him a little while downloading everything from his computer onto an external hard drive for us to go through if we want to. Ya know, to see if there are any of his buddies to take care of. And then I wiped any evidence of Clarice from his searches."

"Good job, Seth," Corbin says, looking over at me with a reassuring expression.

"From what I see, there will be no question he's involved in the arms deals, and it'll lead directly to the warehouse. They'll be able to track everything from the flight plans of every weapon shipment in the last fifteen years, down to every employee on the roster— Oh! Girls, check this out," he interrupts himself.

After a minute, there's a cacophony of laughter.

"What's going on?" Corbin calls over all their voices.

"I'm tapped into the home security system across the street from his house. We're just watching his pitiful attempt at escape after the FBI just busted in his door," Seth replies before bursting out in a fit of laughter. "Oh my God, I'm so saving this so y'all can watch when you get back."

"How much longer?" Clarice's voice fills the vehicle, bringing a smile to my face.

Suddenly, excitement and need overwhelm me as I realize just what's waiting for me when I get back. "Not long, lover. Maybe forty minutes," I tell her.

"And we have the whole club to ourselves, big guy. No masks needed… Knight," she purrs, apparently unperturbed by the fact she's surrounded by all my friends.

"Brown chicken, brown cooooow," Seth singsongs, and I roll my eyes, ending the call as he starts singing "The Bad Touch" by The Bloodhound Gang before I have to hear him get to the part about doing it like they do on the Discovery Channel.

"I have an idea," I tell Corbin. "When you go pick Vi and the kids back up, will you show Clarice to Private Room 2? Tell her I said to wait for me there."

"No problem," he replies, and I hear a smile in his voice, so I turn to look at him, seeing his smirk.

My brow furrows. "What?"

He shakes his head. "Oh, nothing."

When his smirk turns into a grin, I growl, "Whaaat?"

He chuckles. "Nothing, man. I just know what's in Private Room 2."

I can't help but smile. "Yeah. And she's been taking classes. Should be hot as fuck."

He reaches over and claps me on the shoulder. "Can't tell you how happy I am for you, bro. 'Bout time you got some happiness of your own."

"She's been my happiness for eleven years," I remind him.

He shakes his head again. "It'll be different now. You'll see. You don't know what happiness is until you fall asleep every night with the woman you were put on this earth for, your ring on her finger—and if you're lucky, your baby in her belly."

I give him a lopsided smile. Knowing everything Corbin and Vi went through, it chokes me up seeing him have everything in the world he's ever wanted.

"I'm sure you're right. And starting next month, I'll get to experience the first part, when she moves in with me. I just gotta figure out a way to accomplish the second without actually popping the question." When we began our drive home, I'd confided in him everything Clarice had told Doc and me during her second session, after I'd excitedly told him she would be moving in. He asked why it had taken so long for all this to finally happen, and there was no way for him to understand without the whole story.

"Well, bud, as you know, I'm the fucking king of proposals," he gloats.

I roll my eyes. "Yeah, since you've had lots of practice popping the question to the same woman twice."

He flips me off. "Hey now, I'm trying to help you out here."

"Let me think on it a bit. If I can't come up with something, you'll be the first person I ask for advice," I tell him honestly, because, in all actuality, his proposals were pretty fucking epic.

"Deal," he says, just as I pull in behind my SUV at my house.

"I won't be too far behind, so make sure to get her to the private room as soon as you get there."

"No problem, bro. You have fun tonight. Enjoy using our club for the first time, and make it rain." He winks.

"Plan on it." I hop out of his truck, giving him a wave as I head inside to change.

Chapter 17

Clarice

He survived.

I told Brian I love him, told him I'll move in with him, and after going on a dangerous mission to take out a serious threat, he lived to tell the tale. Granted, there have been no yeses involved, at least on my part.

As I sit here in this beautiful room, its gorgeous cobalt blue walls with silver and black accents, rows upon rows of delicious-looking floggers lining one, and black leather furniture the other, I can't help but let my mind wander as I await his arrival.

There have been no yeses from my mouth. Mine.

So what if I were the one to propose to Brian? I mean, he's used to me taking control anyway. It wouldn't really shock him. And in the end, it would be him saying yes, so that would bypass the curse, right?

There isn't anything in this world I wouldn't give to be Mrs. Brian Glover. And I may be thirty-seven, but we still have a little bit of time if we want to have kids. I smile at the thought, imagining a miniature Brian. Goodness, I'm sure it wouldn't take long before he outgrew his momma. So it's a good thing I excel in taking control. Plus, he'd grow up seeing how his hulking daddy treats his mom, no matter how much bigger he is than her. He'd be raised to become another gentle giant.

Or what if it were to be a little girl? A girl with blue-green eyes that sparkle like the sea. She'd grow up seeing exactly how a man should treat a woman, and then she would know not to accept anything less for herself.

Yes. In this moment, I decide yes, I want to marry Brian. I want to have his babies. And if I have to be the one who pops the question in order to make sure we get our happily ever after, then tradition and propriety be damned. I just need to figure out the perfect way to ask. He deserves nothing but the best, because he is the greatest person I know. And I can't wait to make him mine forever.

Brian

I send Seth a text, *"Closer in da Club Remix" by Nine Inch Nails and 50 Cent on repeat in Private Room 2, please.*

I receive a smiling devil emoji in return then immediately hear the hard bass start pumping behind the curtain of the room I stand outside of. I chuckle, shaking my head at Clarice's startled squeal of "Oh, shit!" And when I pull back the curtain far enough to walk inside, she's sitting on the leather cushioned table in the middle of the room, her hand to her chest, looking around for the hidden speakers.

When she turns to me, she takes me in from head to toe and back up again, that plump bottom lip of hers pulling between her pretty white teeth as her chocolate eyes turn molten. She crosses her legs, seeming to unconsciously rub her thighs together at the sight of me in a suit. She's used to seeing me in jeans and T-shirts, camo, or maybe even a nice button-up shirt, but she's never seen me in a suit. The look she's giving me makes me want to fall to my knees before her and give her anything she wants, but no. It's my turn to dominate. I earned my reward, and it would disappoint her if I didn't take it.

So, I saunter over to her, keeping my steps measured when all I want to do is swallow the space between us in quick strides so I can feel her against me. When I stand before her, she uncrosses her legs and sits up straight, a small smile on her pink lips and heat in her eyes. She waits for my first instruction, as she always does when we come to a BDSM club. But this is our first time in my club, and I want us to do something memorable.

I cock an eyebrow at her, putting on an arrogant air, and pull the folded stack of hundred-dollar bills from my suit's jacket pocket, holding it by the silver money clip attached to it. I'd grabbed it out of my safe at home after showering quickly and slipping on my clothes.

"How much for a private dance, beautiful?" I ask her, nudging my head over to the stripper pole on the right side of the room surrounded on three sides by leather chairs.

She glances over and her breath catches for a moment. She hides her smile, lifting one shoulder in a little shrug. "Sorry, handsome. I'm only a cocktail waitress. I don't dance."

I glance from side to side, leaning sideways to look around her body as if searching for someone, before meeting her eyes once more. "I'm sure if I had a word with your boss, we could work something out." I hold up the clip of hundreds, thumbing through the bills.

She gulps, her hands rubbing down the tops of her thighs as she squeezes her full breasts together with her arms. God, she's so good at this. Role-playing with her is my favorite thing in the world. It's why I save it for special occasions—so it doesn't lose its effect.

"That won't be necessary." She slips off the leather table, bringing her flush against me for a moment before sensually brushing over the front of my suit pants with her fingers as she makes her way to the pole. "Please, take a seat," she says, gesturing toward one of the overstuffed chairs.

When I stand in front of it, I unbutton my jacket before sitting down, my knees spreading as I get comfortable. She's sent me all sorts of little videos of her barre and pole dancing classes that she discovered not far from her apartment. The last one she sent, I could tell she was getting pretty damn good, becoming stronger with each class she took. It was seriously impressive since she began with the upper body strength of a kitten and couldn't do a single pull-up.

With the beat of Nine Inch Nails's "Closer" mixed with 50 Cent singing the lyrics to his "In da Club" setting the intensely sexy mood, it's easy to look past the fact that my girl is in her usual leggings and band tee, having not been home since bursting into the house with her discovery in the early evening hours. She slips off her flip-flops, nudging them to the side with her toes, before reaching for the hem of her Killswitch Engage shirt, holding my eyes as she slips it off over her head.

Turning to face the pole, she hooks her thumbs in her leggings and drags them down her shapely legs, bending over so far I can see the line of her black thong between the perfect globes of her ass. I reach down and adjust myself. She's so effortlessly sexy. I'm the luckiest man in the world to call her mine. When she spins back around on her tiptoes, her body is the epitome of the hourglass shape a lot of women strive for. Her breasts nearly spill over the top of her simple black bra, her soft waist curving inward on the sides before flaring once more into generous hips I just want to dig my fingers into while I take her from behind.

She reaches behind her back and unsnaps her bra before letting it fall down her arms. When she catches it, she tosses it into my lap, winking cutely before turning and grasping hold of the pole. And I sink back into the leather chair, doing all I can to keep my mouth from falling open in awe as she weaves her spell with the sensual movements of her delicious body.

Reaching high up on the pole with one hand, she spins and puts her back to it, grabbing hold of it below her ass with her other hand as she lifts her legs to the side. The pole spins on its axis, and she looks like a goddess swirling in the air. Her feet touch the ground only for a moment as she switches positions, facing the silver metal and hooking the outside of her leg around its surface. She takes it in both her hands and lifts herself up, crossing her other leg over the one that's hooked, and it looks as if she's sitting daintily with her legs crossed, spinning above the ground.

Placing her bare feet on the ground once again, she faces me, her upper back pressing against the pole as she does an erotic dance to the music, her naked breasts and the look in her dark eyes making my breath come in and go out unsteadily. She tilts her head to the side, reaching her arms above her head as she takes the pole in her hands, and pressing her shoulder into it. I almost gasp as she throws her legs up, catching the pole with her feet. It sets her in motion, twirling in the air as she bends and straightens her lightly muscled legs in different positions, making her body a kaleidoscope of desire. Every half second, I catch a clear view of her panty-covered pussy as the pole spins, and I don't know how much more of this I can take.

The song ends then restarts, and she climbs down, her breath a little heavy, her skin flushed and glistening with sweat from the effort. She's never looked more fuckable.

Placing my elbow on the arm of the chair, I hold the stack of money between my pointer and middle finger, using my other hand to crook my finger in a "come here" gesture. She takes graceful steps toward me, her hips swaying to the beat, and when she approaches, I pat my thigh. She sits in my lap, her arm coming to rest along the back of the leather chair.

I keep a straight face as I let my gaze wander over her exposed flesh, acting every bit the rich businessman out for a night at a high-end gentlemen's club. When I meet her eyes and with my voice deep and strong, I order, "Dance for me."

Placing a hand on either side of my head on the back of the chair, she stands between my legs and rolls her body, the soft skin of her breasts barely brushing my cheeks as I breathe her in. I keep my hands on the armrests, allowing her to work her seductive spell over me without any hindrance. She grinds her hips, strokes her hands up and down her own curves, her movements hypnotic as she dances to the beat of the hard bass.

When she spins, swaying her hips and making her ass bounce in my face, I can't take anymore. "Thong off," I bark, my hands forming fists. She glances over her shoulder at me. If this was any other time we were role-playing, she'd probably tell me this was a topless club only, playing hard to get. But seeing in my eyes I've gone into full-on Dom mode, my control ready to snap, she obeys without question, looping her fingers around the elastic at her hips and pulling them down her legs the same way she did her leggings. As she bends far and slow at the waist, her feet slightly spread for balance, she reveals her dripping pussy to me, slightly swollen and pinkened from her arousal. I can only imagine how hard she throbs deep inside, and I refuse to wait any longer to find out.

I stand abruptly, my cock pressing against her through my slacks as I grasp her hips where she's bent over. I feel the heat of her through the fabric, and it makes me growl. In one swift move, I pick her up, her light squeal barely audible over the music as I carry her over to the leather table. My need at an all-time high, I don't feel like waiting to use any toys or devices. Not when she's already sweaty and wet with desire. Not when I'm already leaking precum through my expensive suit pants.

I place her on her feet, facing toward the cushioned table, and put the money clip back in my jacket, pulling it off while walking back to where she was dancing for me and laying it across the back of the chair. When I return to her, I put my big hand in the middle of her back, using my palm between her shoulder blades to press her forward until she's lying face down, her round ass up in the air.

I pull my belt from its loops, but before I toss it to the floor like I planned to, I remember her needs. And a good Dom always pays close attention to his submissive's needs. Doubling the belt in my fist, I step to the side, keeping my other palm flat on her lower back. She pants beneath my hand, excitement pouring out of her as she relaxes completely instead of tensing, and her unwavering trust goes straight to my heart and cock.

Rearing back only slightly, because a smooth leather belt is much harsher than the soft, brushed leather floggers she prefers, I whip her right ass cheek, hearing her groan in pleasure. I see her toes curl against the floor, and I can't stop the wicked smile that spreads across my face. Such a dirty girl. I fucking love her.

I give her three more smacks of the belt against her voluptuous ass, imagining her delight later when she sees the stripes across her succulent flesh. She loves it when I leave my marks on her.

I've played long enough. I can't wait a moment longer. Unbuttoning my pants, I pull out my long, thick cock, aching with need as precum drips from the head. Lining myself up with her soaked entrance, I thrust forward, filling her with one hard pump of my hips, her gasp filling me with masculine pride.

Digging my fingers into those irresistible hips, I pound into her, and she reaches above her head to hold on to the other side of the table to keep herself steady. I give in to my desire, her screams of pleasure urging me on as I pummel her tight pussy, sweat dripping down my temples, my teeth bared as I exert all my energy into fucking every ounce of my emotions I felt over the last several hours—anger, fear, anxiety, then relief, devotion, love, and unbearable lust—into her.

"Fuck! Yes, yes, yes…!" she chants, spurring me on, until she finally screams, "Knight!" as her inner muscles clamp around me so tight my eyes nearly cross.

With a heaving grunt, I lose all control, going so deep I hit her cervix as I come inside her. My whole body quakes. The orgasm is so strong, my knees grow weak, so I let myself fall forward, bracing myself on my elbows above her back. With every panted breath, she lets out a short laugh, and I move her hair out of her face to see her smile.

"Goddamn, big guy," she wheezes, giggling. It makes her pussy ripple around me, and I shudder against her, setting off an aftershock of her own.

I pull out gently, threading my arm between her hips and the table, and scoop her up. I carry her back over to the leather chair and plop down into the overstuffed cushions, her body draping across me as we catch our breaths.

"That almost killed me," I murmur, sweat trickling down my back.

She shakes her head. "Nuh-uh. You're invincible, remember?"

"Oh yeah." I nod, breathing heavily through my nose as I kiss the top of her head.

"I mean, you gotta be, if you survived a mission after I told you I love you." She tilts her head to look up at me.

I shrug nonchalantly, giving her a grin. "Told ya so."

"That you did, big guy. That you did."

Epilogue

Clarice

I smile, closing the small velvet box and slipping it into my purse. Finishing up my makeup on my half of the huge bathroom vanity, I prance over to the closet, now stuffed full with my clothes and shoes since I moved in last week. I'm dressed nice tonight, in a little black dress that hugs my curves, showcasing my cleavage. I bypass my usual flip-flops, slipping on a pair of black pumps with two dainty straps with little silver buckles. Even with these heels, Brian will still tower over me, and I fucking love that.

I hurry down the steps, knowing he's waiting for me. We're going to Club Alias tonight, not because he finished up a mission and earned himself a reward, but because he asked me nicely, as if we were going on a real date, not to a sex club. After eleven years, it was surprising and adorable to be asked out by the man I've loved forever. There's no way I could've told him no. Plus, it's the perfect opportunity for me to finally pop the question.

When we arrive a short time later, though, climbing the short staircase inside the entrance, the usual pumping music and sexy couples aren't filling the space. I hold his arm for balance, looking around the mostly empty main room, my eyes land on the booth to the right. Sitting there are all our friends—Corbin with his arm around Vi on one side, Seven snuggled up to Twyla on the other, his hand on her round stomach, and Doc and Astrid sitting close but not touching in the rounded part at the back of the booth.

I look up at Brian, a smile on my face but my brow furrowed. "What's going on?"

Without answering, he guides me over to the booth, gesturing for me to sit next to Vi. He picks up a stack of thick white poster boards from the table then steps back, dropping the first piece to reveal the words on the one behind it.

"Hey, Clarice," I read aloud, and I meet his eyes. "Um, hey, Brian." He drops that piece, the next one coming into view. *"Did you know today is opposite day?"* I read again. I cock my head to the side, a little smile tugging at the corners of my lips. "No, I don't think I knew today was opposite day, big guy."

He grins, letting the poster fall.

"Let's practice," I narrate. *"You think my club is the shit. Yes or No?"* I tap my finger to my chin with a smirk. "Hmmmm, if it's opposite day, then no. I *don't* think your club is the shit." He nods approvingly, switching to the next one. *"You think I'm the most handsome man in the whole world. Yes or No?"* The other guys groan around the table, but the girls giggle along with me. "Most definitely not," I reply with a wink.

But everyone grows quiet when the next poster is revealed.

"You were there for me during the darkest days of my past, and want to be here with me during the brightest days of my future. Yes or No?" I swallow thickly, tilting my head. "No," I say, but every bit of my voice conveys the yes it really means.

Brian drops the last card to the floor, taking two steps to bring him right in front of me before he reaches into his pocket, pulling out a breathtaking diamond ring before going down on one knee. He's so tall it brings us face-to-face. My heart stops as my eyes widen.

"You've been my best friend for eleven years, my lover, my soul mate." He smiles up at me, his breathtaking eyes sparkling in the dim lighting of the club. "It's opposite day, beautiful Clarice. And I chose this day to ask you, will you be my wife?"

Tears fill my eyes as it all clicks in my mind what he's done. And it makes me love him even more for the fact that he would be so understanding that he'd figure out a way to propose without me having to use the word yes.

The tears spill over my cheeks as I let out a laugh before lunging at him. My big, strong, gentle giant doesn't even budge as my full body weight hits him, and he wraps his arms around me as I tell him over and over, "No, big guy. No, no, no." I shake my head before pulling back, grabbing his face, and kissing the ever-loving hell out of him before he slips the ring on my finger.

All our friends clap and cheer behind us, and when I finally stand back up, I shake my head at him, grinning ear-to-ear. "And you wanna know how badly I *don't* want to marry you?"

He stands tall, towering above me, that devastating smile filling his handsome face. "How badly?" he prompts.

I reach into my purse on the booth's bench, pulling out the velvet box and handing it to him. "I was going to propose to you tonight too!" A round of gasps and chuckles circle the booth, and

I turn to narrow my eyes at Seth, who mumbled something about Brian barely hanging on to his man-card. "I knew I couldn't tell you yes if you asked me, so I was going to ask *you* instead. Because there's nothing in this world I want more than to be yours forever," I explain softly, taking a step toward him as he opens the box.

He pulls the necklace out, holding it up to look at it more closely. "Is this…?"

I nod. "Yes. It's the casing of the bullet Corbin used to finally put that day behind you. But it was that day that brought us together, made us inseparable," I tell him, and he rolls it between his fingers.

"It's too dark in here to tell, but is there something on it?" he asks, squinting as his arm snakes around my back to pull me against him.

I nod again, laying my head on his chest, where I discover his heart is thumping wildly. "I had someone engrave a little lock on it. To symbolize a couple of things. The past is now locked in the past, both yours and mine. And as a much *manlier*—" I call loudly, sticking my tongue out at Seth before smiling and looking up into Brian's eyes. "—version of a collar."

"You wanna collar me, Mistress?" he murmurs close to my ear, sending a pleasant chill down my neck.

"Y—" I clear my throat, remembering what today is. "No, my good boy." I reach up and brush his hair off his forehead. Looking into his eyes, I see the pupils almost overtaking all the color as they've filled with so much heat.

He hands me the necklace, bending down a little so I can hook it behind his neck.

And then he swoops me up in his arms, carrying me to the back of the club as we disappear into one of the private rooms.

The End

Want more Brian and Clarice?

Check out my boxed set *Mission: Accomplished*, which contains three novellas of the missions they met up on.

Please take a moment to leave a short review.
Every single one is greatly appreciated!

Join my reader group on Facebook!
KD-Rob's Mob
https://www.facebook.com/groups/KDRobsMob/

Acknowledgements

First and foremost—hubby. For everything.

Rachel, I couldn't ask for a better PA and soul sister than you. Thank you for keeping me organized and taking care of everything (including me) so I could concentrate on writing, and thanks for loving Brian and Clarice so much!

Thank you to my best girlfriends—Jamie, Heather, Erin, Laura, Sierra, and Courtney—for keeping me motivated when my writer's block finally broke. Thank you for pushing me, and making me take a break for a laugh when I needed it. Y'all are the best.

Thank you, Doug (US Army) and Logan (US Marines) for your help getting the Afghanistan flashbacks as authentic as possible. I definitely couldn't have done it without you.

Amanda, thank you for being the perfect muse for Clarice. The ultimate combination of sassy, hot, and sweet. You are truly an inspiration.

Barbara and Becky, I'm so lucky to work with you and feel privileged to have you work on my book babies. Hot Tree Forever. Also, thank you, Chrissy, for volunteering to use your hawk eyes for one last round.

Cassy Roop, you are the poop. Thank you for always being

there for me with your design genius. You never fail to impress the hell out of me!

Thank you, Melissa (my favorite bookstagrammer) and your hubby, for teaching me what a McGangBang was. Your post made my day, and when I read it, I knew it was something Clarice would order in a heartbeat.

Finally, thank you to my Mobsters. Your support never ceases to amaze me.

Made in the USA
Columbia, SC
28 May 2021